Woodworm

Woodworm

LAYLA MARTÍNEZ

Translated from the Spanish by
Sophie Hughes and Annie McDermott

Harvill *Secker*
LONDON

1 3 5 7 9 10 8 6 4 2

Harvill Secker, an imprint of Vintage, is part of the Penguin Random House group of
companies whose addresses can be found at global.penguinrandomhouse.com

First published in Spain with the title *Carcoma* by Editorial Amor de Madre, Malaga in 2021
First published in Great Britain with the title *Woodworm* by Harvill Secker in 2024

penguin.co.uk/vintage

Typeset in 12.5/14.75pt Garamond MT Std by Jouve (UK), Milton Keynes
Printed and bound in Great Britain by Clays Ltd, Elcograf S.p.A.

The authorised representative in the EEA is Penguin Random House Ireland,
Morrison Chambers, 32 Nassau Street, Dublin D02 YH68

A CIP catalogue record for this book is available from the British Library

ISBN 9781787303973

Penguin Random House is committed to a sustainable future for
our business, our readers and our planet. This book is made from
Forest Stewardship Council® certified paper.

To José, so the Devil blesses our wedding day

I

I walked in and the house pounced on me. It's always the same with this filthy pile of bricks, it leaps on whoever comes through the door and twists their guts till they can't even breathe. My mother used to say this house makes your teeth fall out and your insides shrivel up, but my mother left a long time ago and I don't remember her. I only know she said those things because my grandma told me, though she needn't have bothered. It's not exactly news. In here, you lose your teeth, your hair, the meat from your bones and if you're not careful you'll end up dragging yourself around on all fours, or else permanently bedbound.

I left my rucksack on the wooden chest and opened the living-room door. My grandma wasn't there. She wasn't in the larder or under the kitchen table either, so I decided to try upstairs. I checked the dresser drawers and inside the wardrobe but there was still no sign, damn her. Then I saw the tips of some shoes poking out from under one of the beds. I wouldn't normally have lifted the edge of the quilt — you don't disturb what's under the bed — but my grandma's shoes are unmistakable. The patent leather's so shiny you can see your reflection in it from the other side of the room. When I lifted the quilt, she was staring at the slats under the mattress. A neighbour who once saw

I

her climb out of the wooden chest by the front door told the journalists the old woman had dementia, but what would she know, that shit-stirring bitch with her fat-fryer hair. It wasn't dementia.

I hauled the old woman out, sat her on the bed and shook her by the shoulders. Sometimes it works and sometimes it doesn't, and this time it didn't. When it doesn't work you're better off waiting for her to come round. I dragged her into the hallway, opened the door leading up to the attic, shoved her through and closed it behind her, turning the key. All the doors in this house can be locked from the outside. It's a family tradition, like the stupid stuff people get up to at Christmas. We have a lot of traditions, including locking each other away, but we don't eat lamb because lambs have never done us any harm and it feels rude to eat them.

I went down to fetch my rucksack then walked back upstairs. Aside from the stairway going up to the attic, the only space on the first floor is a bedroom I share with the old woman. I put the rucksack on my bed, the smaller of the two. It used to be my mother's and before that my grandma's. In this house you don't inherit money or gold rings or monogrammed sheet sets; beds and bad blood are all the dead pass down. Rage and a place to lay your head, that's the most you'll be left around here. I didn't even get my grandma's hair. It's still as strong as rope, a real sight to behold when she lets it loose, and yet here I am with four greasy strands that start sticking to my scalp two hours after I've washed them.

I like my bed because there are guardian-angel prayer cards sellotaped all over the headboard. Sometimes the tape gets old and yellow and starts peeling, but then I just bite off a fresh strip and replace it. My favourite card is one where the angel is watching over two children about to fall down a ravine. The children are beaming like a pair of idiots, as if they were playing in their own back garden and not on the edge of a cliff. They're old enough to know better, but that clearly hasn't stopped them. When I wake up in the morning I often check to see if the children have fallen yet. There's also a card with a baby about to set a house on fire, another where some twins are trying to stick their fingers in a plug socket, and another where a girl's about to chop off one of hers with a carving knife. They're all grinning away like psychopaths with round, rosy cheeks. The old woman put the cards up when my mother was born so the angels would protect her, and every night before going to sleep the two of them used to kneel beside the bed with their palms pressed together and say their special prayer of four corners to my bed and four angels round my head. But one day the old girl saw angels for real and it turned out that whoever drew those pictures obviously hadn't seen any themselves, because angels don't have blonde curls or beautiful faces. They're more like giant insects, like praying mantises. And so my grandma abandoned her prayers, because who wants four mantises with hundreds of eyes and pincers for mouths showing up at their daughter's bedside? We only pray to them now out of fear they might land on the roof and slide their antennae and spindly legs down the chimney. Sometimes we hear a noise in the attic, go up to see what's going on, and find their eyes peering through the gaps in the roof tiles. Then we say a Hail Mary to scare them away.

I took my clothes out of the rucksack and laid them on the bed. Four T-shirts, two pairs of leggings, five pairs of knickers, five pairs of socks and the black trousers and floral blouse I wore when I went to see the judge. It was the same outfit I wore for job interviews, when I also wanted to give an impression of innocence, virtue and a pretty much total willingness to be brutally exploited. Playing the innocent worked on the judge, but not on the employers. They could probably see the anger in my face because my jaw stayed clenched when I smiled. The only job I'd been able to get was looking after the Jarabos' son, since they didn't care about the blouse or the bad blood. My family had always bowed to theirs and it always would, whatever I wore and however much I resented them.

Now the blouse is too faded to wear, but that doesn't matter because I'm not about to have any more interviews. No one's going to employ me now, not after what happened. So I've been spared having to clock in somewhere each day and grit my teeth to hold down the bile, but even so, the old woman says I'll have to learn to do something. She says it because she doesn't want me hanging around the house all day, but she's also right: if I spend too much time twiddling my thumbs, the jitters and rot set in. One job I know I'd like is dog walking, but who's going to pay me for that? Around here people keep their dogs shut up in pens and those mutts are lucky if someone occasionally tosses a crust of stale bread over the gate.

Anyway. After I unpacked my clothes I took off my T-shirt and changed into a clean one. I'd like to say it was pretty but that would be a lie and I want to tell you things exactly as they happened, and the truth is that both tops were equally ugly and tatty and stretched, but at least the second one didn't reek of the crappy old buses we have around here, with seats that smell like a locker room. I put the clothes away in the bottom drawer of the dresser but I knew there was no point. I'd have to look for them the next day in the kitchen cupboard or on the larder shelves or in the wooden chest in the hallway. It's always the same: you can't trust anything in this house, especially not the wardrobes or the walls. The cupboards a bit more, but not really.

I heard a thud and realised the old girl was banging on the door with her forehead. She must have been coming to, so it was best to wake her before she got near the attic window. This wouldn't be the first time she fell or jumped, and either could leave her crippled or dumb. I went back and opened the door. This time I shook her harder until she fully snapped out of it and said Oh, hello dear, I didn't hear you come in. I told her I'd got back half an hour ago but she'd been gone all that time. When the saints take you they take you, she said, and I watched her walk through the open door and down the stairs. The steps creaked as if they were about to give way, though the old woman must be less than eight stone. The body you see is actually all skin, empty peel with no flesh inside. When I followed her down, the steps didn't make a sound. They can't be trusted either.

The old woman was bustling about in the kitchen, doing twenty things at once. It was almost two o'clock but I wasn't hungry. Back then I was never hungry, I'd just mope around like a sick dog off my food. She put two bowls on the table and brought over the saucepan. There was no need to ask what was for lunch because the menu's always the same in this house. I'm used to it because I've never known any different, but people find it weird which is why I mention it. The old woman's cooking basically involves bringing a saucepan of water to the boil and throwing in whatever's around, normally vegetables from the garden or stuff she finds in the woods, sometimes a handful of chickpeas or beans bought from the trucks that come through the village. The pan bubbles away for hours, then gets boiled up again each day as the old woman goes on adding whatever she likes, and as we eat our way through it she tops up the water and chucks in whatever's to hand and only when the slop's about to go rancid does she wash out the pan and start again. My mother hated this meal, but that doesn't matter because, like I said, my mother left ages ago. I don't love it either but I keep my mouth shut. I'm not about to cook anything else.

I dropped a few bits of bread into the stew as usual and let them go soggy. The old woman took out a bottle of wine and filled three glasses: one for me, one for her and another for the saint. She's not herself, she said, and put the glass beside the little statue of Santa Gema she keeps on an altar by the sink. Then she sat down next to me at the table and asked if there'd been many people on the bus. Only me and the butcher, I told her, and she wanted to know if the butcher had said anything to me with that vile, slobbery tongue of his, a tongue so poisonous he'd drop dead if he bit it. But he hadn't said a word 'cos people round here aren't just vile, they're cowards, and they won't say anything to your face unless they're in a group of four or five.

My grandma got up and poured some more wine into the saint's glass, till it was nearly overflowing. Then she crossed herself. Let's see if Gema will give that bastard bad dreams tonight, she said, but I knew it wouldn't happen because the saint can't deal with every lowlife in this village. Which is why we have to do it ourselves. When we finished eating, I cleared the table and put the dishes in the sink. My grandma went off to the living room and lay down on the bench to pray the rosary. One Hail Mary for the dead, another for the saints and one more for the Virgin of the Mount, who protects the village from high up in the hills.

I went out into the front garden and sat down on the stone bench. The village is always empty at that time, not that the neighbours ever come to our door unless it's to ask the old lady for a favour. When they're forced to walk past the house on the way to one of the olive groves or fields, they speed up as if suddenly remembering they've left the gas on. Though some still find time to spit on the gate. Their gob sticks there and leaves white stains when the sun dries it out. One night someone came and poured bleach on our vine. The leaves all dropped off, but the branches went on clinging to the front of the house. My grandma refused to pull it up. Let them see it, she said, hanging a Santa Águeda prayer card from one branch. The saint's halo and the platter where she carried her severed breasts, amputated in martyrdom, were both coloured in gold. A magpie snatched the prayer card and flew off with it. We left more shiny things out for the magpie, but it didn't come back for them. It was only interested in the saint. Which made perfect sense to me.

I heard a voice calling me and went back inside. The atmosphere had thickened; the house was holding its breath. I went into the living room, but the old girl was asleep on the bench, mouth open, rosary beads in her hand. The voice called again, this time coming from above. I raced up the stairs and reached the bedroom just in time to see the wardrobe door slam shut. I wasn't falling for that one. I pushed a chair up against it and slid the bolt for good measure. Then I turned to leave, but as I reached the hallway I heard a knocking sound. Gentle at first, and then more forceful. The voice was calling from inside, louder and louder. Then came the scratching and the rattling and the wardrobe door was giving way, the wood splintering with every blow. From inside I could hear something like a child crying; I recognised it right away because I'd heard it hundreds of times before. I walked towards it, at which point the chair went flying and the wardrobe door burst open. The whole house huddled around the room, expectant.

Best to keep it shut, dear, said the old woman from behind me. Her voice made me jump. I hadn't heard her come up the stairs or into the room. The voices in the wardrobe always have that effect, sort of stunning you and stopping you thinking about anything else, as if you're deaf or thick or both. The old woman went over to the wardrobe, took out the key she always carries, moved the chair out of the way and turned the key in the lock. The house drew its walls and ceilings around us, pinning us down, either protecting us or smothering us or maybe both, because in here you can't tell the difference.

We heard a car engine stop on the dirt track outside the front gate. I went to the window and opened the net curtain. A flash of light dazzled me for a moment, the sun glancing off a camera lens that was pointed straight at the house. Someone must have tipped them off that I was back. After it all happened, the village was crawling with journalists and the neighbours couldn't wait to tell them the gossip in case it got them on TV. Which it did, of course. The more they ran their mouths off and the more they invented, the more times they appeared. Interviewed live on breakfast shows, they said I'd barely ever turned up to school, that I never spoke to anyone, that they'd never known me to have boyfriends but I used to stare at the girls. Oh, it's hardly my place, but she does sort of eye up my granddaughter . . . and, well, what do I know, but no one around here's ever seen her with a man. That's what those hypocrites would say, the hatred catching in their teeth next to the bits of old food. Like I told you before, it's nothing but fakes and brown-nosers in this village. All queueing up to snitch to the boss the police the journalists about anything at all and never mind what just as long as it gets them a pat on the head.

They came out with all sorts of crap about the old woman as well, saying she talked to herself, slept in the wooden chest and washed stark naked outside under the vine. The interviews kept getting longer and they kept finding more to say. Everyone wanted their five minutes of fame and the more lies they told the more chances they got. The thirst for attention rose in their throats and coated their tongues and all that came out of their mouths was bile and more bile, and it made little difference if it'd been brewing for years or had only just bubbled up. They claimed to have seen the old girl scratching around for bones in the graveyard, or talking to the dead when there was no one else at home. They droned on and on and their gossip and lies were discussed on TV shows and went viral on social media and the whole world thought they knew everything about us. Most people found us disgusting. And they hated us, too, with a syrupy hatred that stuck to the roofs of their mouths and dribbled down their chins while they argued about us on camera. Others felt sorry for us, saying we were sick in the head and social services should come and take the old woman away, and maybe me too, since I seemed a bit loopy or a bit slow or at least not normal enough. I don't care if people think I'm crazy or dumb but as for feeling sorry for me, no way, I draw the line. I didn't do the things I did just to be pitied by that scum.

The old woman pulled me away from the window because she could tell it made me sick seeing the journalists again. I tried to put them out of my mind so I wouldn't get worked up, but I knew they'd be there cracracra in my brain even when I was thinking about other things. I knew it would all come rushing back that night when I was in bed, the bed that had been my mother's and before that my grandmother's and before that I don't know. I heard the boy crying, I told the old woman, partly to change the subject and partly just to say something, since those silent weeks in custody had left me practically braindead. The house has been restless since you got back, she replied, putting an end to the matter. She wasn't one for talking unless there was something that needed to be said. And then, seeing I wasn't satisfied, she turned round before leaving the room and said, You know there are only two ways to calm it down. You can pray to the saints or you can give it what it wants.

Then she tramped down the stairs and I was left alone with the wardrobe again. I could feel it was ravenous, desperate. Like a dog in a pen, like a horse that's been hobbled. When I walked past it to follow the old woman out, the wood creaked. It was goading me into opening the door, the little shit, but I was wise to its tricks.

In the kitchen, the old woman had lit the fire so she could ask it for something. She was feeding it dry weeds and pine branches and old papers. Small portions so it didn't get greedy. As she watched it, she whispered things into the flames. The prayers slid from her teeth and I couldn't hear them but I knew she was calling on Santa Bárbara beheaded by her father on a mountain, Santa Cecilia plunged into boiling water, Santa María Goretti murdered during an attempted rape, and all her other saints who died at the hands of angry men.

When she emerged from her trance, the old lady handed me a prayer card. Give this to the journalist outside, she said, and then she sang the fire to sleep, raking over the embers. It was a picture of the Archangel Gabriel in golden armour with his wings outstretched. He had a sword in one hand and some weighing scales in the other, which I liked because it seemed to be saying there's no justice without death and no death without punishment. What I didn't like was the fact he was handsome and not a mantid or a locust or a moth, meaning this painter had never seen an angel either.

I don't want them to film me, I grumbled, but the old girl didn't care because she never cares what I want. So I set off down the hallway and opened the front door. The house quivered with pleasure or maybe disgust, which aren't all that different. I didn't recognise the journalist 'cos they all look the same to me. Same beard, same hair-cut, same accusing tone. They all make me equally sick.

I crossed the front garden and opened the gate. A

present from my grandma, I said, and held out the prayer card. The idiot stood there gawping, not knowing what to do. I think they were scared of us after all the stories they'd heard, but that suited me just fine. I'd take fear over pity any day. His pal was a bit more with it, and had his camera out and ready. Now the idiot sprang into action as well, snatching the prayer card and grabbing hold of the gate so I couldn't close it again. He spoke to me as I grappled with it, but I didn't hear a word he was saying. My only thought was if I could make him move his hand a little further to the right then I could slam the gate on his fingers. He must have picked up on something because when I met his eye, he whipped his hand away as if he'd been burnt.

Back inside, I heard the old woman in the attic. It sounded like she was lugging around the big copper pots for the pig slaughter. They were all tarnished from disuse but we had no plans to sell them for scrap, since you never know when you might need a pot big enough to fit a little body lying flat. And anyway, that's where the dead like to hide when they turn up here all trembling and lost, and she'd hate to take the pots away and leave them with nowhere to go. They arrive at the house after roaming the hills covered in muck and grime and blood, gibbering wrecks after all they've seen, after all that digging around in those pits, and she'd feel bad if they didn't even have a pot to hide in while they got over the horror.

I went out to the back garden to feed the cats. They hardly ever come indoors in the summer. They prefer climbing the fig tree in the vegetable patch or lying low in the cool of a ditch. Still, they come every day to check up on us and to fill their bellies, because we told them to leave the birds and lizards alone. They get plenty to eat from us, we said, and weren't about to starve. When they saw me, some of them started miaowing like crazy and others came over for a scratch between the ears. I put food in their bowls and then we hung around out there till night fell, 'cos there's little else to do in this house besides stew in your own anger, and I'm pretty sure I've got that covered.

The old woman had laid the table in the kitchen: three plates, three glasses and three pieces of bread on the rubber tablecloth. Your mother seems a bit on edge, she said, so I set a place for her too. I might not remember my mother but my grandma's shown me photos hundreds of times, photos she keeps in the biscuit tin and takes out whenever she gets choked up on grief or anger, which in this house are the same thing. But when she shows me them I don't feel any affection or special warmth or whatever because the girl in the photos is barely half my age and I can't imagine her being my mother. I do feel anger, at least a bit, but I picked that up from my grandma, and besides, it makes me sick that any teenage girl could be snatched away like that with no clothes no money no choice and all anyone knows is that she got into a car and was never seen again.

Once we'd finished I washed the dishes, snuffed out the saints' candles – you never leave anything dangerous within reach of a saint – and went up to the bedroom. The old girl was already asleep, snoring away like a worn-out dog. My clothes were strewn across the floor. I picked them all up, except for the ones I'd seen come sliding from under the bed. If you're caught out once it's not your fault, but by the fourth or fifth time it's a different story, and although that took me a while to learn, now I don't ever forget it. Once in bed, I fell asleep in a flash and didn't wake up till I heard knocking at the front door. The sun had been up for some time but it was still early for visitors. When I got out of bed and went downstairs, the old woman was in the doorway with her hair flowing loose, the way she wore it when she wanted to scare people.

She moved aside and the man came in, but only a few steps. Then he noticed me at the foot of the stairs and quickly looked away. I could see his fear from where I was standing, but I didn't feel sorry for him because it wasn't only fear in there but also pride and scorn. The day still hadn't warmed up but his forehead and armpits were damp with sweat. His lips were dry and blotchy as if he were sick, but he wasn't and I knew it. It was just that mix of shame, fear and disgust that curdled in his throat every time he saw us.

What do you want, the old woman said with all the scorn she could muster on her tongue. He stared at the floor and spoke as if asking for forgiveness, but I knew that if the old woman pushed him a tiny bit more then his pride would come spilling out instead. Emilia sent me to get the stuff for our boy, his exam's on Saturday, he mumbled. I wasn't sure whether to come in case those two journalists were still hanging around, he went on, the words gushing from his mouth now, but in the village there's talk that they overshot a curve and totalled their car last night on the way back to the hotel. And Emilia said she already spoke to you and it just needs picking up.

I moved closer and saw him shiver, a little from fear and a little from disgust, although he tried to hide it. And why exactly would my grandma help you? I asked, right up in his face. It's for the boy, he said, wiping his clammy hands on his trousers. I didn't tell those men from the news anything, he added. Plenty of folks went to them with rumours and stories they'd pulled out of nowhere and Emilia and I said that wasn't right. They came back every single day wanting to know what you were like as a kid and what happened when your mum disappeared. People spouted all kinds of crap just to get on TV, but I said it wasn't right.

I've got nothing for your son but I do have something for you, the old woman interrupted, tired of all the noise, all the lies. She left us by the door and went into the kitchen. The man looked up and met my eye, his pride rising to the surface now, though you could tell he still wasn't ready to bring it out. The stuffy air inside the house smelled of his BO. When the old woman came back, she held out a photo. They gave me a message last night, she said. They want me to tell you they're waiting for you. The man took the photo and frowned, confused. It showed my mother and some other village kids. He was in it as well, a good few pounds lighter but still with that gormless expression. I don't know what you're on about, he said, the pride in his voice fading, and he handed back the photo. Oh, yes you do, my grandma replied and the dregs of his pride drained away, reducing him to a pair of trembling hands, like someone carrying Christ on the cross in an Easter parade. He turned to leave and bumped right into me. His face turned first scarlet then white and sweat was soaking through his shirt collar.

The front door slammed shut, trapping him inside. A gust of soupy air enveloped us. The plates and glasses clattered in the larder and from upstairs came noises like furniture being dragged around and drawers screeching open and shut. The whole house was as furious as we were. You could feel it in every tile, every brick. The man was still paralysed, sweating and trembling but rooted to the spot. His teeth were chattering as if he was cold, though by then the sun's rays were beating down and the breeze from outside felt more like fire.

The old woman laid a hand on my arm and everything that had happened in the last few months came surging through my body. The arrest, the questioning, the mother's tears, the press conferences, the boy the boy the boy. I'd said I left the door open and the boy wandered off by himself said I forgot to close it after taking out the bins said I'd been working for more than twelve hours by that point said I only took my eye off him for a second but by the time I realised, he was gone. It was all rushing back to me.

The security-camera footage of the boy going out by himself, the talk-show guests who said two disappearances in one family was surely no coincidence, the neighbours who said I was a bit slow a bit thick or at least a bit lazy because I hadn't studied or done a day's work in my life before the Jarabos took me on as a favour to my grandma, who'd served them until she got married.

It's all flooding back to me now as well. I'm not sure I can carry on, I feel really anxious but I'll do my best since I'm getting to the end. The old woman said You know what to do, and I did it. When I took the man's arm he was still frozen stiff like he'd seen a ghost, and maybe he had or maybe he'd seen something worse because there are far worse things than the dead when they appear. The knocking above us was getting louder and louder, but it stopped when I set foot on the stairs. I dragged the man up with me and into the bedroom, and then there was a flutter of the quilt and a boot heel vanished under the bed. The wardrobe was open and letting out cold damp air, like fog in a ditch or the gloom of a well. The man began walking towards it, lured by a murmur I couldn't hear though I knew it was there. I could feel it the way you feel power cuts or storms coming on, like the hum of cicadas, only deep in your bones. When the shadows swallowed him I shut the door.

2

After that, for a while, the house was calm as you like. No more creaking or slammed doors or furniture being dragged about. The weeds and shrubs in the back garden even started to grow back, and the brambles came right up to the bedroom windows. The dead settled down as well, giving their muttering under the bed and their wailing in the larder a rest. I hadn't seen any for a few days when one of them whipped out a hand from under the quilt. It was about to grab my ankle but I gave it a good old stamp with the heel of my shoe. You have to keep your wits about you, show them who's boss or you lose their respect and end up dragging them around the house hanging off your skirt.

I should have given my granddaughter a good kicking as well. Or a good clip around the ear. I should have ripped out that thing she was carrying inside before it took root and clamped onto her guts. Heaven's saints and all the lost souls know I tried. I walked barefoot all the way up to the shrine and prayed novenas to the Virgin, but not even she answered my pleas. And now it's too late, I knew it the day she went to work for the Jarabos. My saints had tried to tell me but I didn't want to see. She took that job without a word to me and then it finally clicked. That thing had grown inside her just like it had with my mother, just like it had with me. I tried my best but it's no easy task getting shot of what's inside us. And don't we know it in this house.

When the police arrested her, she fed them the same lies she's told you. That whole story about the boy wandering out on his own and vanishing into thin air. Don't believe a word of it. She puts on that butter-wouldn't-melt act and all those idiots fall for it. So you all had better listen to me because like I say, I know what's inside her. I know what people cart around. I see it, and what I can't see I hear about from the saints when they take me. I know when people are lying, when they want what they shouldn't, when they're resentful and jealous, sometimes even of their own children, their own brothers and sisters. I see the shadows they carry inside.

I can see the shadows in here too. I see them slinking up the stairs and along the hallways, flitting across the ceiling, lurking behind doors. The house is chock-full of them. We've seen some arrive from the village or from up in the hills, but others have been here since the house was built. They got mixed in with the brickwork's mortar and with the lime on the walls. They're in the breeze blocks and the tiles, under the floors and up on the rafters. They kept the house safe from harm for three years of war and forty more after it ended, when life was just hunger and dust and you couldn't tell the living from the dead. When that lot won, they didn't bring their stench around here. They left my mother well alone. But everything has a price, and that's another thing we know in this family. Sooner or later, you always have to pay.

We were spared the knocks on the door in the middle of the night to go for a 'little walk'. But this house is no refuge: it's a trap. Nobody ever leaves it, and those who do always end up coming back. This house is a curse, a curse my father put on us when he condemned us to live out the rest of our years between its walls. And we've been here ever since, and here we'll stay till we rot and for a long time after that.

When my father bought the plot there was nothing here. He got it cheap because no one else wanted to live on a barren wasteland way out of town, not even good for farming because all that came out of the ground were brambles and rocks. There were no other houses nearby. The only things around were the caves carved out of the hillside by people with nowhere else to go, poor beggars who were constantly burying their children. They said they died from fevers but really it's anyone's guess since the only one who ever went there was the priest to give the last rites, and only then if they slipped him a coin, but as for a doctor, never. Sometimes an entire family would be wiped out in their sleep when the hillside collapsed on top of them. Sometimes it was the rains seeping into the soil and making it give way. And sometimes it was the families themselves, digging around in the rock where they shouldn't. They'd be carving a nook for another straw mattress when the latest sprog had dropped, and they'd bring their pick down in the wrong spot. You'd hear the noise all the way in the village, but by the time the locals arrived it was always too late. The hillside had swallowed them up. Mostly they didn't even bother trying to recover the bodies. It was dangerous, for one thing, and in any case no cousin or brother was going to shell out for six or seven funerals. If ever an arm or leg was found poking out from the rubble, the locals would toss on a handful of earth and say an Our Father to send those souls up to heaven. But they didn't get to heaven. No one ever walked past the collapsed caves after that because they all knew those people were still inside.

May the Virgin forgive me but sometimes I don't think God exists because if he did he'd surely have found a place in heaven for those poor souls, who never did anything in their lives but go hungry and slave away for other people. I know the saints and angels exist. I've seen them with these very eyes, and I pray to the Virgin because she always comes good on her promises, except the one about my granddaughter, which I knew all along would be impossible to keep. But how can there be a God who sends those people to hell if hell's where they were already living, cheek by jowl in those caves without a crumb to eat. Maybe that's why he left them there instead of carrying them off to either place, because they'd had their fair share of hell by then but weren't exactly heaven material. Up there it's all bishops and fancy folk who can pay for masses and burials, so how were those beggars supposed to get in? But anyway, those people would stay there under the rubble till eventually one or two would make their way to our house and hide in the larder, where they've been ever since. I don't have the heart to kick them out.

My father never went near the caves, not even when the roar of the landslides woke the whole village and all the men went running to help count the bodies sticking out of the earth. Those people made his skin crawl. He was scared their fleas and their nits and their poverty would spread to him, because poverty's catching too. He despised them with every ounce of hatred in his body, and there was a hell of a lot of hatred in my father.

Much later, when the caves were empty because everyone had upped sticks to the capital to live in different slums, this time under the sky instead of under the ground, I found out he'd grown up in one of those caves. We hate what reminds us of ourselves, you know, which is why plenty of mothers secretly hate their children and why here in this house we've ended up poisoning each other. In my father's case, those poor wretches reminded him of his mother with her hands covered in chilblains from washing other people's clothes in the river, and of his father, who bled to death from a haemorrhage after eating raw chickpeas he stole from a field because it was either that or starve to death. When my father got out of that cave, thanks to a band of sheepshearers who took him on as an apprentice, he swore he'd never go back there. And he didn't, not even for his own mother's funeral two years later. He always stayed true to his grudges.

He crossed the whole peninsula with those sheepshearers. They'd start the season down in Andalucía and end it up in France. Not a bad life for a kid from the caves. When times were good, those fellas frittered away their wages however they could, and when times were bad they caught rats by the river. But my father wasn't into any of that. He wouldn't put up with stinking of barn or pulling ticks off himself. It was better than home, but it wasn't enough. He wanted clean shirts, polished shoes, pressed trousers with a crease down the middle. He was no idiot: he knew only too well he'd never be a gentleman, but he also knew he didn't want to answer to anyone else. He didn't want to shear their herds or till their land. He didn't want to be spoken down to by their children or fetch their kill from the bushes during hunts. He hated the rich as well, you see, but in another way. They didn't remind him of what he was, but of what he'd never be.

In one of those sheep barns, my father made up his mind. He decided to do what all men who hate themselves do: exploit the people beneath him. His whole life he'd thought he didn't have anything, but now he realised that wasn't the case. He had power. True, it was a small and squirming power, a sort of slug that slipped through your fingers if you weren't careful and left a frothing trail of slime in its wake, but it might just get him what he wanted.

First came Adela. She didn't cost him much, just a cheap dress and a bottle of perfume from Cuenca. My father wasn't a handsome man, but he'd picked up a thing or two on his travels from barn to barn. What words to use, what to do. And it wasn't exactly difficult. Adela was just a stupid girl who'd never had anything nice to call her own. I was a stupid girl once, too, but I was lucky enough not to meet a man like my father.

Adela believed everything he told her. That they'd go for strolls arm in arm, that he'd take her out dancing, that he'd buy her sugared almonds and sweets. That he'd go and see her father to do things properly, that they'd be officially engaged and get married at the shrine. That he'd give her children and the eldest would bear his name. She probably even thought he was handsome and didn't mind his crooked nose or thin lips, which were a mystery to his family because the other boys were fine-looking lads, tall and strapping despite all the hunger and hardship. With Adela, my father only needed three months. Then, once she'd fallen into the trap, he locked the door behind her.

With Felisa it was trickier. She wasn't a little girl any-more, she knew men tell lies and lay it on thick and you can't believe even a third of what they tell you. No, the tacky gifts and pretty words didn't work on Felisa. She didn't trust my father, didn't believe the lines he fed her. She was getting on in years and no matter what he said she knew that when he looked at her he saw her droopy breasts, her saggy skin and the wrinkles under her eyes. Why would a man ten years her junior go after her if not because he wanted something? They always wanted some-thing, especially if you were old and past your prime. But Felisa was all alone. She had no family in these parts and she'd lost her husband to one of those fevers that did for all the paupers back then. She'd raised a child alone, one who'd come to her late and frail and cried all day and night, sometimes from hunger, sometimes from cold, and sometimes from a monstrous loneliness that staggered around the house like a chicken with its head half hanging off. Felisa didn't believe my father but she wanted to believe him, and the two things can end up looking alike. By the time she figured it out, the door had been locked behind her as well.

There were others after that. María, who ran away from home when her father beat her and left her with a limp. Joaquina, the maid who'd had enough of the boss's son cornering her in the kitchen to feel her up. Juana, handed over by her own mother because there were too many mouths to feed at home. I don't know if my father really loved any of them or if he hated them all, it hardly made any difference with him. For a while he kept Adela and Felisa in a stable on the outskirts of town. He put in a straw mattress and a basin and made them take turns, while he hung around outside so that no one took longer than they'd paid for or damaged his goods. First things first, the money. He'd charge the punters and then settle up with Adela and Felisa, who always got a raw deal but never complained, in part because they were scared of him and in part because they loved him. Six of one, half a dozen of the other.

A while later he rented the old mill and expanded the business. There were more and more johns and he couldn't keep them waiting because some would get cold feet and go running back to their wives, while others would get drunk and lairy and my father would have to turf them out. All the same, he never had more than four girls working at a time. The demand was there for more, but my father knew the haves don't like it when the have-nots get greedy and without their approval he could never have kept things running. It would only have taken a look, a nod or a word to the right person for the police to raid the business and arrest my father or beat him to a pulp right there in the street, which amounted to the same thing. So, better to keep the rich pricks sweet and not call attention to yourself, not go around in flashier clothes than the ones they wore or with a fatter wallet. A man had to know his place. My father understood that money likes a certain order, it favours a servile smile over a held gaze. I think that's why he married my mother, to maintain the natural order of things, to not raise any eyebrows.

What I don't know is why she did it. Maybe she fell in love with him and believed he'd change once they were married. That's how stupid we women were back then. Maybe she saw her chance not to end up working as a maid in Madrid, where the lady of the house would laugh at her accent when she had her girlfriends over for coffee, and where the man of the house would pity her for being common and simple and tell her to thank her lucky stars they'd given her a route out of the sticks. What I do know for sure is that my mother knew what my father did for a living because in the village it was no secret. Maybe she kidded herself that he was helping those poor women, that he was saving them from being robbed or beaten to death. Maybe she didn't care that he took their money, that he made them believe he loved them and was going to marry them one day. Maybe that was exactly what she liked about my father, that the only promise he ever kept was the one he made to her, that with her it had been true, his 'I'm going to marry you', which he said to all of them. My father was no oil painting, with his bulging forehead and his eyes too close together, yet he'd chosen her and maybe that's what she liked, feeling better than the rest. But whatever her reason for marrying him, she soon regretted it.

This house was my father's wedding gift to my mother. It was a grand building for a village like this, where some people spent the winter writhing in spasms and foaming at the mouth because all they had to eat was grass-pea porridge. But not so grand that the rich set saw my father as a threat, because he always knew how to gauge it just right. The house was beautiful inside, too. My father ordered hand-carved doors, embroidered sheets, furniture brought from the capital. He'd always had good taste, or at least he'd always known how to pick things out to make other people think he did.

My mother loved the house. She'd never lived in a place like that, where the floors sparkled and the walls gleamed when the sun streamed in each morning. The windows let a breeze through and the shutters kept out the summer heat and winter cold. The kitchen was roomy and bright and my father planted a vine right outside the front door so there'd be some shade. But best of all, the house had electricity. My mother had never seen the like, unless you counted her peeking through the lace curtains into the Adolfinas' or Jarabos' houses. It was just a single bulb on a long cable that you carried around from room to room, not a patch on the Jarabos' lamps, which shone like saints' halos, or the crystal chandeliers that hung from the Adolfinas' ceilings, but still, a good sight better than tallow candles with their feeble, half-starved glow.

When they moved in after the wedding, my mother realised straight away that it had all been a sham. The man had lied to her as well. Whatever her reason for marrying him, whether it was pride, love or hunger, in the end she was just like all those other idiots my father had duped. He might have kept his promise, but she quickly learnt that my father was much worse the times when he kept his word than the times when he didn't.

The house, it turned out, was full of shadows. They were inside every brick, under every tile, behind the lime walls, in the mortar. They'd appear every time my mother opened the larder, every time she drew back the bedroom curtains. They'd emerge out of the murky water tank, creep from under the table, sneak down the hall. My mother would hear them breathing next to the bed or crouching behind the door. Oh, San Benito, rid the house of this evil and I'll pray you a novena on my knees, she'd implore. Get rid of it for me and I'll carry you up to the shrine barefoot. But far from leaving, the shadows grew.

Neither San Cipriano, who guards against witchcraft, nor San Alejo, who wards off enemies and jealousies, could do away with them either, though my mother prayed to them every night. Drive out these demons, my Cipriano, she'd say every time she felt one breathing by the side of the bed. But the shadows didn't leave, they spread.

The beatings began on day one. My mother never spoke to me about that but I heard it from Carmen, who herself had heard whispers in the village. Back in the day no one would say that stuff out loud, even if everyone knew. With a bit of luck, your brothers or your father might give the guy a taste of his own medicine to stop him knocking you about so much, like they did with Antonia's husband, who was left an idiot for life from the beating he got in that olive grove. If you weren't so lucky, the men in your family gave you a hiding instead to make sure you didn't cause a scene. My mother's only brothers were two scrawny runts she'd slip the odd cake or loaf to on the sly so they didn't die of hunger, and she was too embarrassed or too proud to tell her father, not that he'd have done anything about it, because she'd been dead to him since the day she married a pimp, and deserved everything she got.

If my mother had believed she was better than the others, my father soon beat it out of her. She was the same as them, with the same bruises, the same fear. He kept those women behind one locked door and my mother behind another. My father hadn't given her that house, he'd condemned her to live in it. It had been built on the bodies of all those women and now my mother's body kept it standing. Her pain and fear. It wasn't a gift, it was a curse.

What my father didn't know was that one day he'd end up trapped inside the prison he was building. When my mother realised she was never getting out of that house, she stopped praying to the saints and started talking to the shadows. Each time she heard them murmuring under the bed or sensed them behind the door she'd sing songs to them as if they were children. Sleep, little darling, sweet dreams lie ahead, your mother's keeping watch from the foot of your bed. Hush, little darling, I'll sing you to sleep, with the sun at your head and the moon at your feet. And the shadows would settle and fall still, and they must have taken a shine to my mother and turned against my father because the whole house would ooze hostility the moment he came through the door. You could feel it in the clammy walls, in the creaking stairs and screeching doors. For the first time in his life my father was afraid. He got rid of the axe for chopping wood, the poker from the hearth, the kitchen knives. He went away more and more often, and sometimes weeks would go by without him spending a single night at home.

But then the war broke out. My father knew he wasn't cut out for the front, since after all, it's one thing to knock about some little bitch but quite another to end up gutted like a slaughtered pig in some filthy hole in the ground. When he was called up, he told my mother to hide him. That night they built a partition wall in the upstairs room, behind the wardrobe. A cubbyhole without doors, barely three metres square, with a small opening near the floor that was easily hidden by the wardrobe. My father climbed inside and my mother plastered and whitewashed the wall with painstaking care, as all important jobs are done.

During the first few weeks my mother passed him food through the hole and changed the bucket of water that he used first to wash and then to relieve himself. He was sure the war wouldn't go on for long, that in a few weeks the coup would wipe out the government, or the government the coup, and he didn't care which because there'd always been whores and whoremongers and there always would be, there's no steadier business than that. But the radio started telling a different story. Madrid didn't fall but the government couldn't take back control of the country either. My father would bang on the wall and rail at my mother, mad with rage locked up in that hole. In the village, the only men left were the old and infirm. Paca's husband had stuck his foot in the fire just so he didn't have to go to the front, but they'd taken him off all the same. His brother had reported him for being a traitor and a coward and they'd come looking for him. Nobody knew where they took him to pay for the shame of being a spineless wimp, but he never came back. My mother repeated these stories to my father through the wall, but he wasn't having any of it. He wanted out of there at whatever cost, he'd walk to France if he had to, hide in the mountains if need be. Now bring me the mallet or believe me woman when I get out I'll beat the living daylights out of you, my father whispered from the other side, and my mother went and slept on the dining-room bench just so she didn't have to listen to him scratching away cracracra with the spoon in the joints in the brickwork all night long. I'm going to rip you apart, you bitch, you won't recognise your own face when I'm done with you, your own father won't recognise you, and then he'd bang the bucket of shit against the wall.

His shouting and cursing grew so loud that my mother began to worry a neighbour might hear. There were eyes everywhere, ears everywhere, even in that wasteland way outside the village where they'd built the house. Then the shadows whispered something to my mother. They put one of their ideas into her head. That night, once my father was asleep, she used bricks and mortar to fill in the rest of the hole. After a few days, his shouts fell silent. My father became another shadow in the house.

My mother gave birth to me five months later. I was born here, in the very room whose walls had swallowed my father. Once she'd recovered from the birth, my mother sold everything in the house. The expensive wooden furniture, the burnished steel cutlery, the embroidered tablecloths. All she held onto was the wardrobe, because the whispers from inside kept her company. She didn't get much for any of it with the fighting still going on and everyone trying to sell whatever they had, but she did get something, especially for the lace she sold to the Adolfinas, who by then were already beginning to sense that they and their kind would win the war. She shared out

33

part of the money among the women who'd worked for my father, and bought a sewing machine with the rest. He hadn't left us anything. My mother searched every nook and cranny but she didn't find so much as a five-peso coin at the bottom of a pocket. She never learnt whether he'd kept his cash somewhere else or just spent it all on expensive shirts and even more expensive favours. With that reprobate, it could have been either.

What my father did leave us was too much pride to ever have a master. My mother wasn't prepared to be a housemaid or spend her days working someone else's land. She had no skills besides cooking and cleaning, but she could learn. She unpicked all my father's clothes and studied the cuts and patterns. She learnt how to sew blind stitches, how to cut the cloth in line with the body, and how to tailor clothes to show off the wearer's best parts and hide all their defects. Later, she did the same with her own dresses and skirts. Within four months she'd become a competent seamstress, competent enough to start accepting customers.

When the war ended, my mother put on her mourning clothes. No one asked after my father, they were all dealing with losses of their own. If you weren't torn apart by one thing, you were torn apart by another. If they didn't come to tell you your son had died in prison, they came to take him for one of those 'little walks'. The Virgin of the Mount knows all about that. She saw the whole thing. Some of them were thrown off the side of the hill up by her shrine. Oh, Mother of Mercy, the way they bounced against those rocks. I can't have been more than four or five but I'll never forget that.

My mother never came out of mourning and never remarried. Only now and then did she let herself relax the rules: a black skirt with tiny white flowers on it, or a blue blouse so dark you could barely tell the difference. She wasn't short of male admirers, though. More than a few came from the village wanting to chat at the garden gate, but she always scared them off, shouting that weren't they ashamed of themselves, sniffing around a widow still in mourning. None of them ever made it through the door. She'd only been with one man in her life but that had been enough. When you're on your own and poor you can't afford to make the same mistake twice, and that's another thing we know all about in this house.

Ever since that night when she bricked up the wall, my mother knew the shadows had got inside her. She no longer just heard them behind the curtains and the doors, but also in her chest and buried deep in her guts. When she put her ear to my belly she heard them there as well. She knew that thing would grow inside us, tangled up in our entrails so we could never pull it out. Everything has a price and that was the one my mother had to pay.

A long time later, when my daughter was born, I used to study her every move. I spied on her as she played with her dolls, watched her as she slept and followed her when she went out. For years I monitored her day and night, listening for any sounds that might come from inside her or slip out of her ears. I'd press my head against her chest, or my ear to her brow, trying to catch the same things I could hear in my head, the same murmur like the sound of cicadas or prayers, the same scratching of fingernails or termites. But I never heard anything. In the end I convinced myself that this thing was inside me because I'd been in my mother's belly when it burrowed inside her, and that it had stopped with me. Oh, sweet Virgin Mary, what an idiot I was.

Then for a long time I didn't think about it, not even when my daughter went missing. I knew who the culprits were, the people who'd have to pay for what they'd done. And this time it was me who'd make them pay, though up until then all I'd done in my life was pay other people's debts. When my granddaughter took the job at the Jarabos' I knew she'd been pulling the wool over my eyes. That thing hadn't gone anywhere. She carried it inside her as well, most of the women of this house carry it from birth, wound around us like a weed that never lets go.

My granddaughter lied to the police and she lied to the judge and she's lied to you as well. She can't fool me with that or with anything else: because I saw it and because I know the rot she's carrying, that woodworm itch in her chest like a horse straining to bolt but it can't, it can't do it, and in the end it gives up. So listen to me, you lot, and I'll tell you what she's not saying. You haven't come here to be told a bundle of lies, I don't care what she thinks. The boy didn't leave the house when she wasn't looking, he didn't just wander off. My granddaughter let him out.

3

A month before it all happened I got toothache, in one of the top molars at the back of my mouth. At first the pain was bearable, kind of like a pinprick or an earwig bite. I tried to get a proper look in the mirror, sticking my fingers in, separating my cheeks from my gums and shining my phone torch inside, but it was too far back. I could see pink flesh and neat rows of teeth all gooey with saliva, but I couldn't see the one that hurt. Then the pain would go away and I'd forget the whole thing and carry on with my life, which was more or less bearable, also kind of like a pinprick or an earwig bite.

But in the space of a few days, the pain stopped fading in and out and instead clamped onto my jaw like those fat yellow ticks you have to pull out of cats with a firm, steady hand. Its tendrils reached up through the roof of my mouth and wound their way into my eye sockets. When I ran my tongue over the tooth it all felt normal, no sour tang of pus, no soft swollen flesh, no hole needing a filling. With my fingers deep in my mouth I prodded around for a gumboil, an abscess, feeling for the sharp edge of chipped enamel, but there was nothing unusual, nothing that could explain that horrific pain.

The old woman watched me whenever I shut my eyes

and moaned and leant on the wall or the doorframe to stop myself passing out. She watched in silence, alert to every flicker of suffering on my face. I felt her eyes on me even when the door was closed, as I was sticking my fingers in my mouth to try and see something in the bathroom mirror. Sometimes they went in as far as the spongy flesh at the back of my throat and then I'd start to gag. I'd keep my fingers there for as long as I could but between each stifled retch came the sound of the old woman edging closer to the door. I'd hear her head brush against the wood, her soft, wrinkly ear pressed up to the varnish, that flaccid ear with its droopy lobe that turns my stomach and makes me look away because one day mine will be exactly the same.

The pain was getting worse. My head felt like it was full of glass shards, full of scissors. I called the Jarabos and told the señora I was sick and wouldn't be able to look after the boy. She said not to worry and to get well soon but from the tone of her voice I knew she was working out how much to dock from my wages. We couldn't afford for me to go to the dentist and besides, there isn't one in the village. There's nothing here but crumbling old houses and crumbling old people, but in the next village along things seem to crumble more slowly and you can still find someone to pull out your tooth. I bought the strongest painkillers they'd give me at the pharmacy without a prescription and by the next day I'd doubled the recommended dose. They didn't block out the pain completely but it bothered me less and everything else seemed to float away, even the old woman's beady eyes, even those revolting ears.

The times when I briefly emerged from the fug of the painkillers, I'd get out of bed and wander from room to room. The house had filled with a kind of haze. Sometimes it was so thick I could barely make out what was in front of me. I'd stumble into things and for a while the pain would shift from my tooth to my foot or my knee or my hip where a dark, dark bruise would form. Other times the haze was more like a fine mist that parted as I moved through it, and on those days I saw the shadows peering down at me from the doorframes and the top of the stairs. I'd not seen so many before or since but the old woman says that yes, it happens, and after the war it was even worse. And on that I'll take her word for it but on lots of other things I won't, 'cos she might call me a liar but she keeps her secrets when it suits her, too.

The old woman started following me all around the house, trailing me down the hallways every time I got up, watching me trip over furniture and feel for the walls and inch my way down the stairs, waiting for me to fall at any moment. She kept an eye on me day and night, even while I was asleep. I felt her presence by my bedside in a never-ending vigil, lurking like a snake or a centipede in the rocks.

One night I woke with a start. I'd taken the same tablets as I had the days before but a flash of pain still shook me from my sleep. I saw her the moment I opened my eyes, and next I felt her cold bony fingers in my mouth. The old woman was hunched over and prodding at my gums my tongue the enamel on my teeth. Digging around inside me with both hands like a butcher. When she saw my eyes were open she pulled out her fingers, wiped the saliva on her nightie, then went back to her bed in silence and lay down. I wanted to get up and grab her by the hair and haul her to her feet and shout what the hell did you do, you old witch, but I was too dizzy. The painkillers had kicked in again and everything was foggy and I could barely move or keep my eyes open. I tried to stay awake because I didn't want the old woman to come back and root around inside me again but it was impossible.

I woke up hours later, well into the afternoon. The sheets were clinging to my body and my tangled, greasy hair was in my face. I'd got so used to the pain that I hardly registered whether it was there or not, so it took me a few minutes to realise it was gone. In its place there was nothing, not so much as an ache. I got up and opened the bedroom door. I felt queasy, like I might throw up at any moment, not that there was anything inside me to throw up because for days I hadn't been able to swallow the old woman's stew, feeling suddenly repulsed by it, having a real thing about it, which was even worse than my lack of appetite from before. The haze in the hallway had cleared, leaving just the same old bitterness and resentment crusting over the walls and floors like a scab.

I searched all through the house for the old woman. The pan was bubbling in the kitchen but she wasn't there, and she wasn't in any of her hiding places, either. The wooden chest was empty and the larder was full of pre-serves she must have made while I was laid up. I didn't look under the bed because I never disturb what's beneath it, but she wasn't there either because the shoes poking out had worn heels and scuffed toes. When I opened the front door and went into the garden, the sunlight made me squint. I'd lost count of how many days it had been since I'd last gone outside. Pushing my matted hair off my face, I sat down on the stone bench. I reeked of sweat and illness and I'd lost weight, you could see my bones jutting out all over.

I was prodding at my ribs when I heard a noise. A few metres from the fence, on the dirt road leading to the house, was a girl. She had on high-waisted jeans and a short-sleeved white shirt, and her straight dark hair came almost to her waist. She looked like a teenager, no more than seventeen or eighteen. She was too far away for me to make out her face but there was something familiar about her, as if I'd seen her before. Everyone knows everyone in this dump but that's not what I mean. She wasn't from here, or at least she wasn't from here and now.

She looked disorientated, standing there in the middle of the road as if she'd forgotten where she was going. She turned back and walked a couple of steps, but then stopped and looked around, unable to make up her mind. She seemed lost, as if she was trying to find something or she didn't even know what that thing was. I went to shout over the fence and see if she needed anything, if I could help her or if she at least wanted a glass of water because at that time of day the sun scorched and spoiled and burnt everything to a crisp. But before I could open my mouth she'd started walking away and then she disappeared behind a sharp rise in the road.

I decided to go back inside. I needed a shower to wash off all the grime and grease and sweat. When I turned around I saw the old woman had hung a new prayer card on the vine. San Sebastián tied to the post, his whole body pierced with arrows, beautiful like a hydrangea, like a volcano. His face cracked with pain, his flesh ripped to shreds, his torso collapsed from the torture, his sex barely covered by the loincloth, and those pleading eyes begging the heavens for mercy or relief or who knows what, maybe even for the revenge that would never be his.

Oh, you're feeling better, dear, said the old woman from behind me, opening the gate. She was carrying a bag of chard and her nails were black with soil but her shoes shone as if they'd just been polished. She looked at the prayer card and then at me and said My saint took your pain away. Sure, I replied just for something to say because I humour the old girl with all that crap but it's not like I actually believe her. Sebastián rids us of sickness and plague, she went on, and anger surged through my body. What plague from outside could ever be worse than what's already in here? I spat, and the old woman fixed me with that gaze that always terrifies everyone in the village like she's seeing right inside you, and in that moment it terrified me too though it doesn't anymore 'cos after what happened, everything's changed.

While I was in the shower, the old lady filled two bowls with stew. I turned it over with my spoon and saw there were chickpeas at the bottom. Hunger had made me get over my weird hangup from before and now I was stuffing my face. When I finished the bowl, I went back for more. By my third helping on an empty stomach I was feeling sick, but I went on shovelling it in all the same. That was when I felt something in my mouth, like a piece of hard smooth bone hitting my teeth. I spat the half-chewed food into my bowl and stuck my fingers in that chickpea mush to pick it out. It was a whole tooth, with the crown and root intact and no sign of any cavity or breakage. I ran my tongue along my gums till I reached the back of my mouth. In the spot that had been sore for all those days, now there was a gap.

Your mother always said this house makes your teeth fall out, the old woman said, getting up to take her plate to the sink. I know, you've told me a million times, I replied, looking away and biting my lip to stop my anger from spilling out. But you've never believed me, she said, and now I did meet her eye. It's not just the old woman who can see inside people. I realised that at the Jarabos' house, when I looked at them and I saw the pent-up rage and frustration and envy in their blood. I could even see it in the little boy.

Did my mother like living here? I asked the old woman. She shut down the conversation with a terse yes, but I could see from the yellowish stain behind her eyes that was another lie. Did she ever tell you she wanted to leave?

I tried again, and then I noticed the old woman start to brim over with hatred as well. Your mother didn't leave, she was taken. I know, but she was young, maybe she wanted to study, to live somewhere else, to get out of this shithole and away from this house, away from you, I said in a rush, like I'd had a grudge stuck in my throat for years and finally coughed it up. I thought the old woman would fly at me, grab my hair and dig her nails into my flesh but she didn't. I could see she wanted to but also that she was broken, crushed. She gathered up the bread and the napkins from the table and put them all in the bread bin. You still don't get it, she said, with her back turned. Get what? I asked, thinking now she really was about to scratch me and shake me and slap me senseless, because the old girl gives as good as she gets. But the beating didn't come. She just looked downcast and a bit angry, just a bit, enough to say: You still don't get that no one ever leaves this house.

That night I barely slept. I couldn't stop running my tongue over the gap where my tooth had been. The tender flesh hadn't yet healed. I felt each tooth one by one to see if they moved, if they'd all come loose by the time I woke up and I'd have to spit them out in the bathroom. How many teeth had my mother lost to make her say that? How many of them had she found in her stew, on her pillow, in the sink?

The next morning I was woken by the sound of the gate squeaking open. I thought my grandma must have gone out early, but when I sat up I saw she was still in bed. I went to look out of the window. Hardly anyone ever comes to the house and especially not at that time of day because the dawn is a time for regrets or hopes, not distress; a time for feeling guilty about the night before or chipper about the day ahead. At dawn the day still hasn't got you latched onto its breast. Almost, but not quite. People only come here when they've tried everything else, when the day the week and even the years have got them cornered and their one remaining option is to have the old woman pray to the saints or perhaps to the dead, though it's all much of a muchness. People think the saints listen to her, but they don't know that really she listens to them.

The girl from the afternoon before was standing in the garden, dressed the same and looking just as lost. She had her back to the house, as if she wasn't sure she'd come to the right place and was wondering whether to stick around. Again, that feeling in my gut that I knew her from somewhere, but I couldn't think where. I felt like I might remember any second, like it would suddenly hit me where I'd seen her before, but I couldn't put my finger on it.

I left the room in silence and went downstairs, then opened the front door, drew back the curtain on the other side and went out. The garden was empty. It had only taken me a few seconds to get down there but the girl was nowhere to be found. I couldn't see her on the dirt track, either, which was now as deserted as ever. There was no way she could have reached the rise in the road so quickly, even at a run. She had to be hiding somewhere. I opened the gate and looked out. But there's nowhere to hide on this barren land, nothing but rocks and thistles and brambles and earth scorched by a burnt-out sun that's given all it had to give.

I retraced my steps back into the garden. When I looked up to tug the outdoor curtain across the pole where it was stuck, I noticed the old woman staring at me from the bedroom window. I wondered if she'd seen the girl, if she'd also had that itching feeling that she knew her from somewhere, that her name was right there on the tip of her tongue only for it to slip back into some crease or nook or cranny.

I went inside and shut the door. The air in the house was thick and heavy, and it suddenly felt several degrees hotter. The wooden ceiling began to creak and the house filled with a sound like power cables like tram wires or like the rails before an oncoming train. Upstairs I heard furniture being dragged around, hinges squeaking, footsteps hurrying to and fro and then stopping and then hurrying back again.

I headed for the stairs to go and find the old woman but when my foot touched the first tread everything stopped. The house fell quiet as if expecting something, as if something were about to happen. Then came a knock at the door. Two raps in quick succession. I went and turned the handle. There, on the threshold, holding the curtain aside and staring blankly ahead, was the teenager from before. Now that I could finally see her face, I realised why she looked familiar. I'd seen her in photos hundreds of times. It was my mother.

4

I've told you before, nobody ever leaves this house. We're trapped here, us and the shadows. That's what my mother used to tell me. We're trapped here till they come and take us, she'd say. Until who comes and takes us? Whoever might come knocking at the door and frighten the dead so hard they go off with the saints.

My granddaughter didn't want to believe it. She thought she'd be able to up and leave the second she was old enough, that she'd go off to Madrid to study and never come back. But in the end she stayed. Where was she going to go? Who was going to pay for her to study in the capital, when only the rich kids do that? She did look around to see if there was any sort of backing for people like her but she soon abandoned that idea. Around here people only give you something if you've got something already and they can take it off you later. And if you've got nothing, that's what they give you, nothing. People like us aren't welcome in the capital to study, only to serve, but even then, maids are ten-a-penny. Can't you see times have changed, my granddaughter would say to me, but really she was the one who needed her eyes opened. We spend our days hunting around for anything to throw in the cooking pot and that lot spend theirs showing off, and it's always been that way. In the end she didn't go to Madrid because at least here she had a roof over her head and food to eat. That's what family is, a place to stay and food on the table and in return you're cooped up with a bunch of living relatives and another bunch of dead ones. All families keep their dead under the mattress, my mother used to tell me, it's just that we can see ours.

But I also see plenty of things that my mother couldn't. Aged six the saint appeared to me for the first time. My mother had gone out to chase payment for some sewing she'd already delivered to the Adolfinas, who were quick to put the orders in but slow to settle the bills, like all the trumped-up bastards who make out they're richer than they are. None of the three sisters had tied the knot because marrying one would be like marrying all three and if they were hard work by themselves then together they were like a prison sentence, and there wasn't a man alive who'd sign up for that. So, dance after dance, the three women remained single and if some guy did have his eye on one of them, the other two made sure to scare him off. They spent their days squandering the money left to them by their father, Don Adolfo, who'd made a killing in Cuba as a slave trader. With the outbreak of war there he'd sent his daughters and wife back, along with his great fortune and equally great passion for slaving, because not even the Jarabos treated the help like they did, with good, clean slaps. The money eventually started to run out and their maids went around telling all and sundry how the sisters mended the moth holes in their dresses on the sly, even though they still lived like the landed gentry. They even had a swimming pool installed with a changing room and everything, the first time anyone around here had seen the like. They asked my mother for embroidered tablecloths and linen sheets, but then she had to nag them for months to get paid, and that's what she'd gone off to do when the saint appeared to me. My mother had left me at home carding wool. I hated that job because ever since I was little I'd found the smell of dead hair disgusting, but my mother didn't care because disgust, like compassion, is a luxury the poor can't afford.

It was late and the room was getting dark, when suddenly it was flooded with the brightest light I'd ever seen. A cold white light, the kind you get in an operating room or airport, although back then no one in this village of paupers had ever seen either. When the baker fell off the mountainside in his cart, they took him back to his house and opened him up right there on the kitchen table, with his daughters looking on. One of those girls was left half dumb from the horror, couldn't string together more than three words after that, but I suspect she'd always been an idiot and what she saw that day just made it worse. The real tragedy, my mother said, was the baker's wife, who was left with a brain-dead daughter and a husband who was no good for anything besides shitting his pants, but who wouldn't pop his clogs either. I can tell you right now if that had been me he wouldn't have been long for this world, my mother would mutter under her breath, and then she'd make me cross myself so the house didn't start its screeching and creaking.

Anyway, I was saying how I closed my eyes for a moment, blinded by that light. When I opened them, there was a woman standing in front of me. She was dressed in a black tunic that covered her from the neck down and her hair was parted in the middle and tied back in a low bun. Her hands were clasped over her chest and her eyes were raised as if she were praying. I was knocked for six by the sight of her and couldn't tell you how long I stayed like that. I only emerged from my stupor when I was shaken by the shoulders and the saint disappeared. My mother had come back from her errand and found me lying on the floor staring blankly at the ceiling. If you don't snap out of it I'll give you to the nuns, said my mother. I've been calling your name since I got in and you haven't even looked at me. And you know full well I don't have the patience of the baker's wife.

The nuns had taken several girls from the village since the war. Some were handed over by their families because they couldn't make ends meet. Others they went and collected on the priest's orders because the parents were either in jail or in the cemetery, which boils down to the same thing. The aunts and uncles or neighbours got tired of supporting the girls and would go to the priest to have him make the problem go away. None of those girls were ever seen again. My mother said they sold them to rich people, the pretty ones as daughters and the ugly ones as maids.

Since then I've seen the saint plenty of times. She always appears to me in the same pose, just like on the prayer cards. Gazing solemnly upwards as if she's listening to

God's orders, poised to do anything for him, anything at all, even go after young girls like I was and scare them witless. She never looks at me or speaks to me directly, but I hear her voice inside my chest and I know I have to do as she tells me. How are you meant to argue with a saint? How can you not do everything they say?

When I told my mother about it, she said I'd better not breathe a word to anyone else. It was to stay within these four walls, just like my father's screams. She never asked what the saint said to me, but she'd stare at me intently every time I returned from wherever the saint took me off to. I could see the envy on her face; she was jealous that I'd been chosen over her, that the only things to appear to her were those shadows in the grip of despair. She wanted a saint to speak to her, inside her chest. She wanted to see that saint shrouded in light and beautiful as a miracle. What had I done to be worthy of that, when I'd never even had to kill a man?

The older I got, the more jealous my mother became. The saint didn't take me very often, though when she did she told me about things that were going to happen and things that had already happened but nobody ever spoke of. That's how I found out that the miller was lying in a grave beside the cemetery wall, that the mayor's son would get kicked by a horse and die, and that I'd watch the youngest Adolfina sister drown and not do a thing to help. My mother's patience for my visions dwindled as her envy grew. Resentment made her cruel and miserly, or maybe she'd always been cruel and miserly and her resentment just drew it out. She forced me to wear her old dresses and hacked away at my hair with the garden shears, cutting out great chunks and leaving it shorter on one side. She also made me drop out of school. The teacher told her I was bright and could even go and study in Cuenca, that the nuns ran a residence there and she could have a word with them about lowering the price because she was a widow, but my mother refused. I've never gone begging and I'm not about to start now, she said.

When we got home from talking to the teacher, she told me to freshen up in the washtub and go and ask for work from the Jarabos, who were looking for a maid because one of theirs was about to get married. You've always said we'd never serve those people, I protested, anything but serving you said. When you know how to do something else, you can get yourself a different job, my mother shot back, but I'm done being sponged off. That was my punishment. To serve the people my mother had refused to serve, to bow before those my father had refused to bow to. To obey on behalf of my whole family.

I served for nine years in that house, between the ages of ten and nineteen. The couple were civil enough to me and Carmen, the other maid, but every so often the mask would slip to reveal the hatred lurking beneath. Like when the señora ripped up the coats she no longer wanted so we couldn't reuse the fabric, or when the señor forced us to remove every single stone by hand from the dirt road leading up to the finca so he wouldn't get a flat tyre. It was an age-old hatred they carried inside, so deep it took no effort to express it. It wasn't fuelled by anger but by contempt.

We, on the other hand, were full of anger. It ran in our blood like a fever. I don't know if Carmen passed it on to me or I passed it on to her. Sometimes I think it was her because she'd been there longer and was older, but other times I think it was me because I brought all that bad blood from home. Either way, we stoked each other's hatred. She'd tell me the suits the tailor dropped off at the house were worth twice our monthly wages, and I'd tell her the señora had poured two full bottles of perfume down the sink because she only liked the ones they made in Paris. But it was the eldest son we really despised. He studied law in Madrid, where he cosied up to all the right people, men who talked about modernising the country and whose mouths, on speaking of their beloved Spain, filled with blood. He came back every summer because he liked the hills and going out hunting. Carmen and I would see him in the doorway, a load of dead partridges hanging from his belt, and hatred would spread through our guts like a disease. A few years later he was killed in a car crash and his parents buried him in the family vault, the biggest in the entire cemetery. The youngest son was still a child but you could see he was already spoiled.

Sometimes the señora made us cook the partridges the eldest shot. We had to pluck those birds with our bare hands and every single time we'd almost die of sadness and disgust. But of laughter, too, later, as we watched the family mop up the sauce we'd spat in. Old Carmen would hawk these great big globs that floated in the oil and then we'd stir them in with a spoon. You just can't beat a lovely piece of game, the señora would say, and behind the kitchen door Carmen and I would have to hold in our snorts.

I think that's what cemented our friendship – gobbing in our masters' dinner. She'd grown up with hardship but with love as well and you could tell from her character. She didn't have that gnawing restlessness, that woodworm my mother and I had, that bastard itch that won't leave you in peace or let you leave others in peace either. Her father had learnt to play the bandurria by ear, just by trying and trying, and he livened up the romerías and fiestas and delighted all those who went to his house to dance and drink the night away. Her mother was quieter but she knew a lot of songs. If you pushed her, eventually she'd sing them for you, first in a hushed voice, blushing, but then she'd find her stride. Carmen had grown up around dancing, and I around effing and blinding, and how could that not leave its mark? I hardly saw my mother anymore. When I came home in the evenings after clearing away the Jarabos' dinner plates she'd already be asleep, and in the morning we'd barely exchange two words. She was making me shoulder my whole family's punishment but even then the envy went on chewing her up inside. That's when I knew she was never going to forgive me. It drove her wild with rage that the saint came and spoke to me instead of her. And she couldn't stand the way I knew about a lot of things before they happened. That I wasn't surprised when the mayor had to bury his son after his liver packed it in or that they found the youngest Adolfina sister drowned in the swimming pool shortly after I returned from her house on an errand for the Jarabos.

My mother's resentment only grew when I met Pedro. He showed up one day at the Jarabos' door, drenched in sweat and smeared with soot. A fire had broken out at the señor's warehouse in Gascueña and all the contents, including some of the recent grape harvest, had been destroyed. Pedro took a seat on a kitchen chair to wait for the señor, who was due home at any minute. I moved the clay water jug closer to him and went out into the garden. The mule he'd arrived on was wheezing, struggling for breath. He must have whipped her hard to hurry her along. I led her into the shade and brought her a bucket of cool water from the tank. Don't worry, that animal can take it, came a voice from the door. You shouldn't have pushed her so hard, what difference does a few minutes make if the warehouse has already burnt down? He wandered over to the mule and stroked her back. Everything they own can go up in smoke for all I care, but then I'm the foreman, he said, and if he finds out from anyone else that he lost a small fortune today, he'll beat the shit out of me and I'll never work again.

After that visit there were plenty more. At first he'd find excuses for coming to the house to deal with matters that until then had always been handled in the winery, but then he stopped pretending. He'd saunter in through the kitchen door and sit watching me shell peas or mix cakes. Carmen usually just smiled and left us to it, but one day she took me by the arm and said that Pedro had a girl-friend; she'd heard he was due to marry a girl from Gascueña and the whole wedding had been arranged. I already knew. The saint had told me, just like she'd told me he wasn't going to marry that girl, that the person Pedro would marry was me.

He came to see me every Sunday, when the señora gave Carmen and me the afternoon off once we'd tidied the kitchen and left dinner ready. We'd meet at the edge of the path, head into the woods and come back with our clothes covered in dirt and sweat. Tongues started wagging in the village, as they always do – those bastards can never keep quiet. Carmen told me I'd been spotted coming down from the hills with tousled hair and flushed cheeks, and that they all knew I'd been going home via the woods instead of the main road, well after dark. But then, what could you expect from the daughter of a pimp who lived off women? I'd suckled the milk of a shameless mother, for all that she liked to play the respectable widow, year after year spent in mourning clothes as if she came from an even halfway-decent home.

One afternoon I led Pedro to a natural pool among the rocks and took off all his clothes. I'd never seen him fully naked; I'd only ever guessed at the hidden parts of his body while reaching my hands under his shirt or down his trousers. I liked his strong chest and broad back, and he liked my hunger and desire. I lay down on the ground and let him do as he pleased. He enjoyed having my body to himself. I already knew what was going to happen, I'd seen it on the kitchen ceiling. That afternoon I fell pregnant.

Pedro didn't want to marry me, but he never said so. He assumed his responsibility without reproach or blame and with his head held high, the way he did everything else. And he loaded his things onto his mule and came to live in the house with my mother and me. I stopped working for the Jarabos before I started showing to spare them the scandal of a pregnant maid. Pedro was still their foreman and he needed to stay in their good books. We got married at night and without any guests. There was no reception or banquet, there was nothing to celebrate about our disgrace. My mother made my dress, black for mourning and wide for the shame.

5

The old girl's right, I never really believed I was trapped in this house, however many times she said it. I always thought I'd get out one day, that I'd put this crappy village behind me just like everyone else. There was no one my age left around here because anyone who could went off to Madrid, and anyone who couldn't went to Cuenca, some to study and others to work on building sites or in supermarkets or at Zara or basically anywhere as long as it got them out of this dump full of half-dead geriatrics. That's what I thought but then I realised that no, my grandma was right all along. The women in this family only leave when we're forced, in my case when they locked me up and in my mother's when they took her.

So, I was at the part where I saw my mother at the front door. She didn't open her mouth or even look at me, more like through me and out the other side. She made as if to come in so I moved out of her way and she stepped into the gloom of the hall, treading softly, as if to avoid making a sound or waking anyone up. She walked past me and headed for the stairs. When she turned, a lock of her long dark hair brushed against my arm and a shiver of warning or maybe more like confirmation ran down my spine. I knew she was my mother and I also knew that, where she'd come from, that didn't matter.

The old woman was watching from the top of the stairs. Silent, like the rest of the house. I had the feeling she might pounce, that she might swoop down on us, but she didn't. She just stared at me the way she always did, trying to force my thoughts from my head and replace them with other ones. Sometimes she managed it. I'd hear her digging away cracracra in my brain and then suddenly I'd be thinking things I wasn't thinking before. She's stopped doing it now. She doesn't need to. After what happened, we have an understanding.

My mother reached the foot of the stairs and began making her way up. The old woman turned from me to her but her face showed no emotion. She looked like one of those huge glossy spiders that hunt mosquitoes by the water pump in the garden, staying still still still as can be till at last it's time to spring out and swallow them whole. She wasn't surprised that my mother was back. Maybe she'd also seen her wandering around on the dirt road, or maybe the saint let her know, just like she told her the name of the person who took her daughter away and the exact point on that same road outside where all trace of her was lost forever. Or maybe my grandma had seen so much rot in her life that not even her own daughter returned from the shadows could make her bat an eyelid.

At the top of the stairs, my mother walked past the old woman and into the bedroom. I came round from the shock and followed her up as fast as I could. The house was still silent, expectant. The old woman's right when she says this house is a trap, like the snares those bastard hunters set in the woods and forget all about so that for years they lie hidden in the undergrowth, just waiting for the moment to slam shut.

I went into the bedroom and saw my mother standing in front of the wardrobe. The wood creaked and the whole thing inched forward very slightly, greedy, straining. And then before I could do anything she'd stepped inside and the door closed behind her with a thud. When I opened it, there was nothing there but my grandma's mothballed skirts and blouses. Don't worry, the old woman said from behind me. She hasn't gone anywhere.

I started rummaging through the wardrobe, more out of frustration than anything else, when I heard another two sharp raps downstairs. Someone at the door. My guts were in knots and my heart started to pound like a bolting horse. It was the same knocking as before. I hoped the old woman would open the door, since she'd gone downstairs while I was yanking drawers open and shut hoping I'd find my mother's face staring up at me from the bottom of one. But then I heard her in the back garden, on the other side of the house, calling the cats, so I went down and hovered by the front door. Even before I opened it, I knew it was her.

She repeated the whole thing step by step. Walking in through the door without looking at me, going up the stairs and then into the bedroom, opening the wardrobe and disappearing inside. This time I didn't go after her, I just stood there gaping like an idiot. From downstairs I heard the wood creak and the hinges whine and the door slam shut again. My mother had never been more to me than a teenager in an old photo or an oath on my grandma's lips. She wasn't even an absence because she'd never been a presence, but now she was back as if she'd never disappeared, or as if she disappeared every day and every day we were forced to feel our hearts ripped out again. And with that I did start to feel a tiny tiny little absence, like a hole.

I heard the old woman and came back to my senses. She was inside again now, pottering around in the kitchen. The house was so quiet I could hear her shuffling to and fro and muttering curses at one of the shadows that lived in the cupboard and must have reached out and pulled her hair. You swine, I'd kill you if you weren't already dead, she was saying, though fat lot of good it would do to threaten a shadow that's dragged itself here from the deepest corners of hell. After a while the old woman came into the hallway. She walked straight past me and out the front door, which I still hadn't shut because my body was hunched up with pure terror and had stopped obeying orders. She took a rosary from her skirt pocket and hung it on a branch of the vine that climbs up the front of the house.

Rage flooded my body because I realised my grandma must know something and she was keeping it to herself and she'd been keeping it to herself for years. Is that to make her leave? I hissed, wanting a reason to be the one to pounce this time, the one to swoop down like a giant insect. You know there's no getting rid of them but at least this way they don't cause a nuisance, the old woman said, before coming into the house and closing the door. I gripped her arm hard, my insides churning and the hole expanding into a trench a pit a crater. What's she doing here? Why did she only just come back, after all this time? She didn't only just come back, the old woman said, pulling her arm away. I let go and followed her into the kitchen, rage coursing round and round my body and spewing out of my mouth. What do you mean, she didn't only just come back? The one thing stopping me from flinging myself at the old woman and scratching her weasel face was that I needed her to answer, to tell me what she wasn't saying. She's been coming back for years, she replied. Since right after they took her.

I sat down at the table and pushed aside the saucepan the old girl had taken off the stove, ready to wash before starting the stew again. Some of the dregs slopped onto the tablecloth in a greasy puddle that made me retch. Why haven't I seen her till now? I asked. My anger had turned to nausea or sadness or something else, I didn't know what, but the urge to scratch her had gone. Who's to say why we see what we see, she said, or why some shadows are just a wheezing sound around a corner and others are furious vermin, why sometimes they appear as the faintest of shivers and other times they burrow deep in our guts. She slurped from the wooden spoon and some cold broth dribbled out of the corner of her mouth, leaving an oily trail down her chin. Now she didn't look like a majestic insect but like any little old lady you might feel sorry for and maybe find a bit disgusting, but not frightening, not even close.

I left the kitchen, went up to the bedroom and lay down on the bed. On the other side of the room, the wardrobe seemed calm. No more clattering and creaking. I couldn't see my mother anymore but I felt her there, like a breath or a sigh that flitted past me again and again, crossing the room and disappearing into the wardrobe. If I listened closely I could hear footsteps coming up the stairs, the creak of the door handle, the squeak of the hinges. I shut my eyes and noticed the air in the room stiffen. Then I felt one corner of the bed sink slightly, as if someone had sat down there and the mattress had dipped under their weight. I opened my eyes right away and sat up to look around for my mother, but all I saw was a lock of black hair disappearing under the bed.

When I was little they were always catching me out with those tricks. They'd lure me in with their happy songs and I'd lift the quilt and follow them under the bed, and a few hours later I'd be back in the room with my skin covered in scratches and my clothes all torn, the fear lodged deep down inside me but with no idea why because I couldn't remember a thing. Now I knew it wasn't my mother who'd sat on my bed or slipped out of sight beneath it. My mother hadn't come back to take care of me or watch over me as I slept or to stroke my hair in my dreams. She hadn't even wanted me, she was just a stupid teenager who got knocked up by someone she shouldn't have and gave birth to a baby she'd never asked for. It wasn't my mother I was seeing, it was what was left of her after the hell they put her through when they took her away.

When I woke up the room was in semi-darkness. The old woman must have pulled down the shutters before she went to sleep. I didn't know how many hours it had been but my pillow was soaked with sweat and my belly tight with hunger. The air still hung thick and heavy like the air in a basement or a room that's been shut for so long that when you open it up all the things inside are still where you left them only they're not things now but shadows of themselves.

I got out of bed and went into the hallway. The old woman was downstairs praying the rosary, you could hear the murmur of the sorrowful mysteries. First betrayal, then torture. Then coronation, crucifixion and death. Mary Mother of Grace, Mother of Mercy shield us from our enemies. Send your angels upon them, parch their fields, make their wheat grow without kernels and their vines without fruit and give them no rest, not even in death. I went down to the kitchen and into the back garden, not wanting to be anywhere near the front door should my mother knock again. I didn't want to watch her repeat those movements over and over like the old woman had been forced to for years, the old woman who'd been left without a body to bury but only that pain that torture passing again and again before her eyes. Give them no rest beloved Virgin for we ourselves have none.

I wanted the house to keep hiding my mother from me like it had all this time, for the whole thing to be just a reflection I glimpsed through a half-closed door and then for that door to slam shut and never open again because what was behind it was the old woman's business, not mine. It could gnaw away at me, yes, but only so far, not like the great chasm inside the old woman because it was her pain her guilt her sadness her innards ripping tearing rending, her daughter's body still in some ditch or pit or bramble patch while the person who'd done it got away scot-free.

Once I'd noticed the chasm inside her, all her grudges and cruelty, all that meanness and bitterness began to make more sense. And that must have latched onto me somewhere and started to grow because when I went back to the Jarabos' after being ill it didn't feel the same. The boy behaved the same, the mother treated me the same but I couldn't stand them anymore, I just couldn't. A darkness filled my body and it spread with every day that went by. And the old woman must have noticed because one morning she said the time had come and I knew she was right, that it had.

I spent all that day with the boy. I'd got there at nine in the morning and now it was past midnight. Neither of the parents was back yet. The mother had called before leaving Madrid. She'd just had dinner with her girlfriends and was about to get in the car, so she'd be home in an hour and a half. She sounded a bit tipsy, her voice higher than usual. I hated that voice, those plummy drawn-out _S_s, those over-the-top *D*s to avoid speaking like us proles with our cansao and comío where we should say cansado and comido. I wanted the car to crash or skid off the road, at least give her a scare. The father wasn't back either but he hadn't called. He never did.

The boy had been impossible all afternoon. He was one of those brats who'll have a tantrum over the slightest thing, but that day he'd been worse than usual. He'd thrown his lunch on the floor, chucked a glass at my head and destroyed the bouquet of roses his mother had arranged on the dining-room table. I was sick of putting up with him, sick of the crappy wages, sick of his parents treating me the way their family has always treated mine, their voices dripping with disgust and condescension like all rich people when they speak to the help.

I could have punched him, could have slapped him in the face for being stupid and spoiled. I could have locked him in the bathroom with the light off till he either shut up or cracked his head open on the sink, but I didn't say that to the police. To the police I said he's a restless child with an independent streak, which is what teachers at posh schools tell the parents of unbearable children and those parents think it means their kid's going to revolutionise robotics when really it just means no one can stand them. I said I'd been trying to get him to sleep for an hour but it hadn't worked at all. I said at eleven I decided to leave the room and get some air. We were both frustrated and tired, so I thought I'd leave him with his toys for a few minutes and then go back and give it another shot. I went downstairs and took out the rubbish. It was hot, the night was heavy and dry and there wasn't any breeze. When I went back inside, I headed to the fridge for a cool glass of water.

I told them that must have been when I left the front door open, but that I didn't remember. I was in the kitchen for a while, looking at my phone. The boy's mother had called at half past ten, so it was another hour before she'd be home, and I still hadn't heard from the father. I checked my WhatsApp but there was nothing. In all that time I didn't notice any noises in the house, nothing out of the ordinary. When I finished my water I went back to the bedroom to put the boy to sleep. He wasn't there. I called his name several times and looked around his room and then his parents' room. I thought he was hiding, playing some game because he still wasn't tired. I looked all over.

I told them I tried the ground floor next, searching the dining room and kitchen in case he'd gone down while I was looking upstairs. I don't know how much time passed but it can't have been long. I thought he'd jump out at any moment, but I still didn't stop looking for him. Crossing the entrance hall I realised the front door was open. I went out and looked in both directions. You don't get many cars up there, but I was worried about him being outside by himself. I started shouting his name, then walked several metres down the road each way and checked the bushes and dustbins in case he was hiding there. I could feel myself getting more and more anxious.

He'd hidden from me before, but never outside the house. I said that was when I called the police.

I said it all very calmly, with the short sentences and full stops and commas they love so much, exactly as I'd written it that morning. They made me go over it again and again with different questions and I always answered the same, just changing a word here a detail there so it wasn't obvious that I was doing it from memory, that I'd learnt it off by heart. And I must have done a good job because a few hours later they let me go home but then after two days they called me again and said I had to go down to the station and then I really did get twitchy because I couldn't remember it all anymore and didn't know if I could say it the same way. I saw from their faces that something was off, and that time they wouldn't let me go. Since they didn't have anything on me, I think they were trying to make me sweat to see if I might let something slip. But I stayed as cool and calm as I could in that cell because they had no way of knowing I left the door open on purpose or that I tricked the boy into going outside or that the old woman was waiting in the road, ready to take him away.

6

All the women in this family are widowed quick. The men burn out on us like church candles and not long after we're married all that's left of them is a stain on the sheets that won't come off for all the scrubbing in the world. My mother used to say this house dries them out from the inside. And she should know, because when we removed a brick to see my father he was crisp as esparto grass. I must have been about eight and I'd come home in a rage because Matilda's youngest had told me my father wasn't killed in the war, he'd run off with one of his tarts. What do you care what that goody-goody says? my mother replied. Does she think we don't know how many people were taken on 'little walks' because of her family of snitches?

I slammed the door as I left the kitchen, snarling and snapping like a dog. My mother followed me out and grabbed my arm, digging in her nails and pulling me towards the stairs. I'll show you where your father is if that's what you want, don't you worry, she muttered as she dragged me up. When we reached the bedroom she let me go and heaved the wardrobe away from the wall. Then she hoicked up her skirt, knelt down by the wall and pulled out a loose brick four rows from the floor. There he is, she said.

The house had eaten his flesh but left his skin, which was sticking to his bones. He had a funny look on his face, I remember it as if he were right here in front of me now. He was sitting on the floor with his back against the far wall. His head had flopped to one side and his mouth was hanging open, as if he'd dislocated his jaw. It looked like he was screaming in agony. He's got no eyes, I said, turning away from the hole. He doesn't need them in there, my mother replied, and she pushed me out of the way.

My mother had loosened the brick two years before, once the victors stopped sniffing around for the men who'd left home to escape the war, because by then they'd killed them all. Even those hiding out in the hills, picked off one by one like roe deer. Since then, not a day had passed when she didn't look in on my father, to reassure herself that he was still there. That agonised look on his face never failed to make her smile. Then she'd put back the brick, push the wardrobe into place and make the sign of the cross. May death bring him all the suffering he should have been dealt in life.

My husband also dried up from the inside out. He wasted away in bed the same year we got married. He grew weaker and weaker and before long he couldn't even move. The flesh fell from his bones and his skin turned yellow. My mother and I had the doctor out plenty of times, whenever my husband was burning up, but he could never decide what was wrong. He'd give him an injection, charge me a small fortune and then leave the way he came, abandoning the poor man to his fits and ravings. I knew none of that would help, the saints had told me as much, but Pedro had always been a gentleman with me and I wasn't going to let him die like a dog.

The Jarabos paid for the burial. As a token of appreciation for their foreman, they said. I saw red when they took centre stage at the funeral. The señora even managed a few tears. Plenty of people offered *them* condolences. I'm so sorry for your loss, they said, as if that family had ever lost anything. That's when they took a dislike to me. The señora noticed the way I looked at her. Someone must have told them what I'd said at the service, that if they really cared about their foreman they'd have paid for his medicine, not his burial. I wasn't bothered, I said it good and loud so that anyone who wanted to could hear. They should have got a doctor down from Cuenca if they appreciated him that much. Or from Madrid, one of those they met at their dinner parties with the Generalissimo.

The señora began to despise me with a hatred she usually reserved for the kinds of people worthy of her attention. Not the disdain she'd had for me when I was her maid, but a deep loathing she didn't try to hide and that only grew as the days went by. I preferred her loathing to her indifference because at least then I could give her something to hate me for, but it's also true that hatred brings trouble in its wake. She started making up stories, hinting that we'd done something to Pedro, saying he'd been a healthy young man till he walked through our door. She'd whisper this stuff to anyone who'd listen, telling them we must have put something in his food, insinuating that he wasn't the father of my daughter, accusing me of getting pregnant on purpose to stop him marrying his girlfriend.

It wasn't as easy for her to hurt us now that I didn't work for them, but with that mouth of hers she poisoned everything she could. Those suck-ups in the village stopped talking to us, as if whoever received the most pats on the head from the master would magically stop being a dog. Of course I didn't let her get away with it. If they thought I had it in me to kill my own husband, I'd at least give them reason to believe it.

First I dealt with the señora. I asked Carmen to bring me a few strands of the woman's hair from her hairbrush. She slipped them into her apron while cleaning the dressing table and turned up with them the next day. Let's see if we can't make that viper bite her own venomous tongue, she said. My mother and I put the hairs inside a handkerchief and tied it up tight. With every knot we prayed to a saint. To Santa Dorotea who came back from the dead with a basket of flowers and fruit. To San Dionisio who carried his head in his hands. To Judas Iscariote who hanged himself from a fig tree. To Santa Gema who saw angels and dead people like we do. Then we dug a hole in the garden and buried it there so nobody would find it and undo the knots.

My mother had never made one of those bundles before, but she'd seen her mother do it once, after her boss slapped her in the face for knocking over a glass while serving dinner. The next day, when he went to

74

mount his horse it kicked out and almost killed him. The animal had never given him any trouble before, but something had got into it that morning. The horse left his insides so mangled the doctors had to stitch up his guts. The man ate nothing but soup for the rest of his life and still he writhed in pain each night.

We made our bundle to the best of my mother's memory, using her prayers and the tightest possible knots to stop anything from escaping. Nothing happened the next day, or the day after that. How are they meant to find it buried down there? I said to my mother. Then I went out into the garden, dug it up and left it in the bedroom wardrobe. Two days later, the señora fell down the stairs and broke her ankle. Carmen couldn't contain her giggles when she told me how she'd shrieked. But the shadows weren't finished yet. The next week it was the son who fell while out hunting, breaking both wrists. Down in the bar his friends described how he'd been following the sound of a large animal in the bushes, a snorting they all thought came from a wild boar, and he'd ended up falling between some rocks without finding any trace of the beast. A few days later a fire broke out in the señor's study while he was away and all the papers he kept locked in a drawer were destroyed. If the señora hadn't smelled burning, Carmen said, the whole house would have gone up in flames.

In the village, people started to talk because you can put one accident down to chance but not two and definitely not three. Three accidents in the space of a few days means there's bad energy behind it, no matter how much the señora played it down and said it was nothing. Well, it didn't seem like nothing when she was screaming like a banshee, Carmen said as we waited in line for bread, and all the other women tittered. Some of those same women started coming by the house after dark, wanting to use a bit of that bad energy to sort out their own unfinished business, of which there'd always been plenty, and even more so since the war. They would sneak out of the village over by the haylofts and cut through the woods so nobody saw them. Some wanted to get revenge for a smack or a beating they'd been stewing over since the carnage that came after the war, others for a neighbour grassing them up or for the time their relative tried to flee and it turned into a manhunt and then into a massacre. I put curses on relatives, policemen, priests, informers, whoever, with all the hatred in these guts of mine, and in the house's guts too, because I knew that once we poor folk started collecting our debts they wouldn't have so much as a pigsty to hide in.

Later on, some of them started coming round asking for cures and I'd give them the two or three herbs I knew about and tell them one truth and one lie to keep them happy. The truth was always the place where their disappeared father, husband, daughter or sister was now. Along the cemetery wall, the road to Villalba, the ravine, the hill with the shrine. The whole village packed full of bodies. The lie was that this father, husband, son or sibling was in heaven, that the saints had told me they were up there with them and that they sent their love. Then I'd let them stay there and pray with the saint and light a candle for their relatives because they couldn't go and get their bodies and bury them or ask the priest to say a mass. So they'd sit in the kitchen and I'd light the fire to make sure they didn't get cold, and the lie would cheer them up a bit, even if it meant that the shadows they'd brought with them stayed at the house with their mouths full of dirt or their heads full of holes or their teeth knocked out with a rifle butt. Some of those shadows would disappear after a while, and in the end maybe the angels did come to raise them up to heaven, because kids who bleed to death in ravines with their guts hanging out can hardly end up in hell. But the others hid in the pots and under the beds, out of fear or anger or who knows what, and they never left.

I didn't charge for disappeared relatives, but I did charge for remedies. If it was something small I'd give them a fistful of salt to spit in and throw at the door of whoever was bothering them. If it was something more serious, I'd make up a bundle and put it in the wardrobe. The house liked it when I did that. The angrier they were with the person they wanted to curse, the better the bundle worked. I charged a fair bit so they didn't do it for any old nonsense, but half the time they had no money anyway, and they'd bring me monogrammed bedlinen, wedding rings, pots and pans, all kinds of stuff. I never accepted any of it. My heart broke just thinking about sleeping on sheets stitched with other people's initials or wearing other people's wedding bands, and in any case, we were earning enough to get by. My husband hadn't left me any money because he was useless when it came to all that. If I'd been the foreman, I'd have worked out how to squeeze something out of the Jarabos when they weren't looking. I wouldn't have broken my back running their winery for a pittance while they stuffed their faces with pastries and sirloin steaks. But my husband was too cowardly or too honourable, the two worst things a poor man can be.

All I was left with from our marriage was a baby girl who cried a whole lot and got sick even more. She was forever getting fevers I couldn't bring down or coughing fits that would have her crib shaking. My mother was sure she was going to die. So many children died back then, you had to baptise them quick because just like that they'd catch a chill and by the morning they'd be cold as icebergs in their cribs. But my daughter didn't die. She pulled through every fit and fever with the grit her father had lacked. This girl wants to live, Carmen used to say when she came over to see us. And I never told her, but it wasn't that. The thing is, in this house the dead live for too long and the living not long enough. Those of us in between, like me and my daughter, do neither one thing nor the other. The house won't let us die, and it sure as hell won't let us live anywhere else.

I was sorry when Pedro died because he hadn't treated me badly. He got on with his work, never raised his voice or his fist, and I never saw him come home looking shifty because he'd been with other women. You can't ask much more of a man. Maybe, at a push, to not get in the way, and he didn't do that either. He ate what was put in front of him and was silent more than he spoke. Love me? He didn't love me, any more than I loved him, but we were fond of each other and he liked that I never stopped wanting to rip off his clothes at night.

After I buried my husband, the girl carried on growing into an ugly, scrawny thing. So skinny it looked like she'd come from an orphanage, no matter what we fed her. She was yellow as wax and all shrivelled up like a little baby mouse, bald and covered in wrinkles. Mark my words, Carmen would say, ugly babies always grow into beauties. I didn't know whether to believe it. I was scared the house had done that to her, that it was the shadows' fault she'd turned out like that.

As I say, I kept a constant eye on her as she was growing up. I watched her every move, didn't leave her alone even for a second. I'd spend whole nights awake beside her bed, which we'd pushed up against my own. I was looking for a grimace, a moan, something to tell me if the shadow was growing inside her or if it was all in my head. My mother, meanwhile, barely went near her. She felt the same disgust for her as she had for me, the same resentment she'd had latched onto her guts for years. She was afraid the saints would visit the girl too, that my daughter wouldn't be bound to the shadows like she was.

As time passed I could see that Carmen had been right. The girl got less scrawny and hunched as she grew, her puffy eyelids and bags disappeared, her skin lost its sallow tinge and her hair became thick and dark. By the age of six she'd turned into a beautiful girl. What did I tell you, Carmen said one afternoon when she came round to see

79

us. Carmen had a lot more afternoons off then, ever since the señora caught wind that when she wasn't working in her house she was often at mine. But the señora didn't dare fire her, no matter how bolshy Carmen got, or how loose her tongue became. The señora hadn't forgotten about that bad energy, you see, and every day she made sure to remind herself about our reputation for cursing people with bundles. Once, to her horror, she found Carmen cleaning her dressing table and ran over to snatch back the hairbrush. Someone must have told her we used hair in our bundles and she'd worked the rest out for herself. After that the only one allowed to clean her room was Margarita, a dopey girl who joined the house when I left and who used to prattle on in the shop queue about the señora's great taste and the elegant fabrics she had sent from Paris and the superior embroidery, not to mention the lace she had specially made. Would she still look elegant if she dressed like us, or would she look more like the old dog she is? I asked in the queue, and some women laughed and others turned away so their names wouldn't be mentioned when the gossip inevitably reached the señora. Most likely those suck-ups were thinking of scurrying off to tell her themselves, to run into the señora outside mass as if by chance, as if they hadn't spent the whole week hatching their nasty little plan.

The girl grew more and more beautiful while my mother steadily wasted away. She developed a bulge on her hip that made her walk with a stoop and meant she had to grip the banister with both hands, practically dragging herself up the stairs. What little meat was left on her bones disappeared and she lost all her teeth in just two months. Wrinkles formed on her skin from one day to the next. She looked much older than she was. I don't know if her own bitterness was finishing her off or if the house had simply got bored of my daughter and decided to have some fun with my mother instead. Whatever it was, I didn't mind seeing her suffer. I couldn't remember ever feeling anything but resentment towards her. Maybe as a child, before realising that she gave me those awful haircuts on purpose, or when she pulled me out of school and sent me to work as a maid, to clean up the shit that the rest of my family had refused to touch. Every ulcer she got and every tooth she lost felt like payback for what she'd done to me, a personal gift from the saints or the devil, and I didn't care which.

When she died I slipped the gravedigger a tip so he'd put her in the grave facing the wrong way, with her feet up by the headstone. I wanted to send her a message about what would happen if she tried to come back home. It was only Carmen, my daughter and me at the funeral. My mother didn't have any family left and no one else from the village had wanted to come. The man crossed himself but then pocketed the money and got on with what I'd asked. And I don't know if that's what did it, but she never came round here again.

7

My great-grandma died when all the hatred finally gob-
bled her up, just like it did her husband. He ended his days
walled into the house he'd built to imprison his wife, while
she was consumed by jealousy towards her own daughter.
They both died of sheer loathing sheer contempt sheer
bad blood. She was right to leave him there behind that
wall, reduced to the cracracra of a spoon against brick,
but that cracracra got inside her head because in this
house everything gets inside you and scratch scratch
scratches away.

Hatred finished off the rest of the family as well, but
other people's hatred, not their own. My grandad wasted
away in his bed after a year in this house because he
couldn't hack the malice that dripped off the ceilings. We
women grew up here, but my grandad didn't and he wasn't
cut out for this shithole. All he left behind was a ring of
sweat and piss on the sheets and that baby girl who grew
into my mother and who also died as a result of other
people's hatred. That's what does for everyone in this
family. It might be their own or it might be other people's,
but it's hatred every time.

The old woman's right that we get eaten up by anger,
though it's not because we're born with something twisted

inside. It twists up later, bit by bit, from all that gritting of teeth. I realised that when I started working for the Jarabos' grown-up son, who'd moved to the village with his second wife to take over the winery after his father and brother died. That first day, as soon as the boy's mother opened the door, my jaw began to clench. How could I not get twisted up inside, how could I not start to fester and grind my teeth? The moment I saw her there in the doorway I knew I shouldn't have come, but where else would I find work in this dump? There's nothing to do here but pick grapes for a few weeks or wipe the shit off some old bastard till he falls down dead or they put him in a home. Better to look after a kid than an old man, I thought. It's enough of a morgue back at ours.

Angustias' daughter María went for the job as well. Her mother had been sick with something all her life, but not even the doctors could work out what and whenever María pushed them they tried to tell her it was all in her head, as if she hadn't seen her mother near-on paralysed after one of her turns, barely able to speak in her distress. María had stayed at home to take care of her mother since her father couldn't be trusted to boil a potato and her brothers had gone off to university and never come back. But my boys worry terribly about me, her mother would say to the neighbours who'd call round to see her when she couldn't even move. They phone every week. And I don't know if María saw red whenever she heard her mother say those things, while she herself scrubbed the bathroom or mopped the kitchen floor, but it was enough to make anyone bubble over with rage and throw the pail of dirty water in the old cow's face and drag her by the hair from room to room to see if the brothers had made the beds or cooked the lunch.

After Angustias died, when the brothers next phoned it was to put the house up for sale. They'd buried the father a couple of years before and now they wanted to sell what they had left in the village. María couldn't afford to buy out her brothers so they sold the place to strangers instead and left her on the streets with five thousand euros in her pocket. From one day to the next, María found herself with no home no pension no dole and no brothers, since they never called again. For a while she rented a house from a neighbour in the village and worked the odd grape harvest. When she applied for the job I got, she didn't stand a chance. Eventually she could no longer make the rent and got taken away, and no one ever laid eyes on her again. Word had it she'd lost her marbles and ended up in an asylum.

When she'd turned up at the Jarabos' house I'd thought they'd take her instead of me, since she was significantly older and needed the work more. But when Angustias died María was already over sixty and those people don't like frumpy old bags with DIY haircuts. They're fine for the grape harvest because that's all they've known, working like donkeys all their lives for a pittance, but not to have at home looking after the children. Those people don't want their little darlings brought up by some poor hick with market-stall clothes and visible roots because

what could she possibly offer them if she'd never had anything, never amounted to anything herself? How would
she show the boy his place in the world and the import-
ance of money and success, how would she teach him to
walk over others when she'd only ever been walked over?

The boy's mother had looked us both up and down and
given the job to me because she knew when her city
friends came to visit they'd wonder how much she was
paying and who'd given my references and how many languages I'd speak with the boy. I'd never taken care of a
child in my life and only knew a bit of English from school
but that didn't matter, what mattered was that I didn't
look like a pauper a peasant a dunce who'd done nothing
in her life but scrub floors. What mattered was that her
friends would see me and think I must be charging a tidy
sum. I could tell all that just from the way she looked at
me. On the TV they said someone should have called
social services because I'm not right in the head but
they're wrong about that 'cos, when you think about it,
I'm still here at home after everything we did and who else
could say the same?

The old woman blew her top when she heard I was
going to work for the Jarabos. Apoplectic, possessed, she
yelled in my face, You think they picked you to show you
off but really it's to humiliate you. I don't know what I said
to that but deep down I knew it was true, that everyone
would think my knocking on their door to ask for a job
was proof we'd been defeated, that the son had finally
won the war my grandma had waged on the señora and all

her family when she insulted them at the funeral in front of the whole village and made everyone think she'd set fire to their house and broken their bones with her bundles.

How could my grandma not be furious with me when she'd had to suffer those people's scorn all her life, when even as a child she'd been expected to look at their shoes instead of their faces, when she'd had to listen to people offering them condolences after her husband's death? How could she not have a belly full of rage when, after all that, she saw me go crawling to their door to ask for a job, saw I was going to look after a Jarabo son and raise him to be yet another bastard who'd look down on us yet another rich prick who'd inherit the land and the vineyards and the right to make us work them in exchange for a handful of coins? And as if that weren't enough, she'd been condemned to see her daughter's shadow around the house day in day out and year after year.

I only understood where the old woman was coming from once I started work in that house which had belonged to the father and now belonged to the son but hadn't changed a bit, because nothing ever changes around here and the one time people rose up and tried they were beaten to a pulp, bludgeoned to death, taken off to the hills and shot in the mouth. I thought I was smarter than she was, that the old woman's grudge was just hot air, old news, and that I'd finally get the money together to leave this house and never come back. But at the Jarabos' I realised what an idiot I'd been, that it was true they'd hired me instead of María to impress their friends, but they were more than capable of flaunting me and hating me at the same time, like someone showing their guests a hunting trophy or a wild animal in a cage. They liked the city set thinking I must be costing a fortune, while in the village people knew I was working for peanuts, because that meant everything was as it should be again and we'd all been put back in our place.

My great-grandfather had refused to serve them and they'd turned a blind eye, but only up to a point and only because they'd recognised something of themselves in him: the urge to crush whoever's beneath you. They knew he was no threat to them because his kind never look up the chain, they never target anyone higher, only those below. And they're handy to have around because sometimes you need to impose order and they're the ones who'll take aim and shoot where you tell them, the ones who'll stop at nothing. But as for the old woman, they'd never forgiven her for insulting them in front of the whole village, or for making everyone think that with a few strands of hair and a couple of prayers to a saint you could send the señora plunging headlong down the stairs. That was something they could never forgive, something they absolutely couldn't allow because then all the village riff-raff would think they could do as they pleased, that they could threaten them, break their leg or arm if they felt like it, just by saying a little prayer.

Now I was working for them and they could make it clear that order had been restored and the old woman was just a crank who'd swallowed her own stories, her own lies. Having me working there was proof. I'd done my bit, I'd played my part in showing the whole village that the Jarabos had won this time just like every other time, and the old woman had put up with all those insults and slights over the years since the funeral for nothing because sooner or later everything falls back into place. I thought about quitting, about walking out so she wouldn't be reminded of it every single day, since the damage was done but there was no need to rub it in her face. Then one afternoon, with the words on the very tip of my tongue, just as I was about to say That's it I'm leaving, the woman told me some clients were coming to the house and I was to stay with the boy in the bedroom and make sure he didn't come out and disturb them. The clients always went straight to the winery but sometimes they ended up in the house for some reason and when that happened I was told to shut myself away with the boy in case he had a tantrum and everyone saw what a horrible brat he was. If anyone asked she said he was in a French lesson or practising the piano.

But that afternoon there was no keeping him in his room, not even for a few minutes. Over time he'd caught on to the fact his mother wanted him out of the way when she had guests, which made him even more intolerable. He yelled insults and pulled my hair and threw everything he could find at me, biting and kicking me when I tried to make him stop. When I couldn't take it anymore and my body was itching to hit him I gave him my phone to play with. That usually worked because his mother never let him have hers. But that day not even the phone made any difference. He flung it out of the open window and ran off down the hall. By the time I caught up with him he'd reached the living room, where his mother was holding forth about the artwork in the house.

Well now who do we have here, said one of the clients, a woman, in that idiotic tone of voice adults use when they talk to children. You must be Guillermo. The boy held out his hand in a charming imitation of a grown-up handshake and everyone burst out laughing. Have you finished your French lesson already? No, I replied, taking the boy by the hand to lead him away, we just came for a glass of water. They didn't even wait for me to leave, didn't hold off for a few measly seconds till I was out of earshot. The problem with language teachers who aren't native speakers is the children end up with an accent, said the same woman. It's awful, the mother replied, but it even happens with Spanish. He repeats what he hears from the girls who help in the house. My husband and I thought it would be a good idea to raise him out here in the countryside for the early years, with the horses and vineyards, before choosing a good school, so he wouldn't spend all his time staring at a screen, but the other day he said comío instead of comido and I swear I almost packed my bags there and then.

I heard them laughing away for a long time. And I could still hear them after they left and when I put the boy to bed and came back home, that laughter on a loop in my head.

The muffled snort of someone pretending to hide it, pretending they don't want anyone to hear when really that's the whole point, that sneer like a landowner tossing a coin on the ground or a farmer watching his pigs at the trough.

That was the night I finally understood everything. It all rushed into my head as I was lying in bed. The old woman had always thought the Jarabos' hatred was one of those long-standing feuds between families that fester and fester and never form a scab, but it wasn't. The Jarabos weren't any worse than others like them and they didn't hate us any more than they hated others like us. They'd taken against the old woman because of the bundles, because now the whole village thought they could wish ill on their family and get away with it, that they could slip through the woods in the middle of the night and come to this house in the middle of nowhere, in the middle of a wasteland, to cook up some bad luck for the boss the lord the master without ever paying the price. But they detest us all equally, find us all equally disgusting, and that disgust gets inside us and fills us with a poison that we carry so deep down we start thinking it's ours, but it's not. And then I fell asleep and when I woke up the rage was gnawing away at me like woodworm and I don't know if the shadows put it there between whispers in the night or if it came into my head of its own accord but that doesn't matter because either way I knew I had to get it out. I couldn't quit my job just yet. There was something I had to do first.

8

Of course I didn't like her working for them. How could I be pleased she was looking after the son of those bastards who'd destroyed our family? Oh, she was very careful not to tell me what she was up to till after they'd given her the job. She knew I'd have taken her by the scruff and locked her in the woodshed before letting her wait on them in that house. I'd have sooner killed her than watch her become their nanny.

Needless to say, the Jarabos hired her on the spot. They could have picked poor María, thrown out on the street by her brothers, those mean bastards, you'd have to be dead inside to do that to your own flesh and blood. But no, the Jarabos chose my girl. She thought it was because she was younger and easier on the eye, and I'm not saying she didn't have a point, that the snooty missus, the second wife of the new lord of the manor, wouldn't have deemed María too ugly for the house. God sends these people and they find each other and this new wife was the same as the first one or maybe even worse, only much younger. But deep down I was sure the husband hadn't forgiven us for throwing him between those rocks when he was out hunting that time. In public, the Jarabos laughed off the rumours and said they'd all been chance events, but behind closed doors,

Carmen told me they weren't so sure of themselves. She had begun clinging to the banister and he now kept his rifle under lock and key.

Come to think of it, I'm not sure if he was holding a grudge about the accident or if what he couldn't forgive was the whole village thinking I'd caused it with a few little prayers, as my granddaughter puts it, though it boils down to the same thing. He'd held on to his bile for all that time and now he had an outlet. She went knocking on his door because to her mind a job was a job – you were always working for someone so what did it matter who. She just wanted to save up enough to get to Madrid. But once inside that house she found a lot of things started to make sense. She went in with one set of ideas and left with another. I'd fly off the handle every time she came home, knowing the villagers would be thinking that after all these years we'd finally dragged ourselves back there begging for work, but then my granddaughter started opening up and telling me the ideas she was having in that house. I already knew a lot of the things she told me, but I'd never put them all in order like that. I wish I'd seen them sooner because then I could have told my daughter and maybe she wouldn't have disappeared. My granddaughter says we can never know, that maybe she'd have disappeared all the same, that there was nothing I could have done. But I can't help feeling that if I'd seen things more clearly back then she and I would have understood each other better, we wouldn't have shouted and she wouldn't have walked out, slamming the door behind her.

My girl was very beautiful. Not like us two, who are short and hipless like weasels. No curves to speak of. She was tall and lovely, graceful as a deer. That shrivelled, yellowish baby had turned into a stunning young woman and when she walked down the street the whole town turned to look. She was a real sight for sore eyes. The local women used to talk in the bakery queue, asking how such a pretty, warm-hearted girl could have come from a house like this one. That's what Carmen told me. Those miserable bints were quite happy to bad-mouth us, but that didn't stop them coming knocking for favours later on.

In any case, the worst stuff wasn't what the women said but what the men came out with. Carmen couldn't tell me about that because they kept it between themselves. I heard it from the saints instead. They told me the men would boast about what they'd do to my daughter, some with desire and others with hate, which men often mistake for desire. The saints recounted it word for word, sparing no detail, and I'd try to remember what each of them said. And remember I did. I stored it all inside this head of mine.

I told my daughter some of it, but she didn't believe me. She said I was just trying to scare her to stop her from going out, to keep her cooped up with me within these four walls. She told me people in the village laughed at me, that they called me crazy and made fun of me behind my back. That she was embarrassed to be my daughter. And I knew all that too. I knew she laughed about me with her friends, telling them how she'd find rosary beads under the bed and little bags of hair between the sheets. I knew she told them I talked to myself and that I believed the saints appeared to me every time I had a funny turn. She'd send me up worse than anyone so her friends would see she was different, that she had nothing to do with her mother and didn't believe those old wives' tales.

The saints told me all this, but there was no need. She made quite sure that everybody knew, me included. There were other things she didn't want me to know but the saints used to tell me about them as well, when they took me. They said she'd go with the boys to the threshing grounds to drink and smoke and listen to a radio that belonged to the Jarabo kid. By then almost all those boys had left the village, some to study and most to work, but they came back in the summer. After my daughter disappeared the visits stopped, but for the two or three summers before that they all came back the moment the holidays began. They spent their days lazing in bed and their nights out partying, going off to the fiestas in nearby towns and coming back drunk as skunks, driving along the godforsaken roads we have around here, all winding and potholed. None of them died because it wasn't God's will.

My daughter hadn't wanted to study. I wouldn't have been able to send her to university, because who can afford that, but I suggested a vocational course which she didn't go for either. She'd just about scraped through school, though she hardly bothered to show up to class. She used to tell me she couldn't handle sitting there for hours listening to all that crap that didn't even apply to anything.

She couldn't hold down a job, either. When she did sometimes get one in winter she'd stick it out for a few months, but she'd always quit when the summer came around. If she didn't have enough cash to go out, she'd find someone to pay for her. There was always a guy willing to buy her a drink, plenty hoping for something in return, others demanding it.

Quite often it was the Jarabo boy who paid her way. He was a few years older than her, he'd studied law like his brother and landed a job at a firm in Madrid, but he liked the old ways here. Here that reprobate could hunt and go out riding in the hills. The saints told me he often had an eye on my daughter, and a lustful eye at that. I lost my mind just thinking of that little shit going after my girl. That family was never satisfied, they always wanted more. It wasn't enough that we worked for them, that the entire village slaved away in their vineyards, we had to get them off as well.

But I won't lie to you, my daughter got a kick out of him running after her. The stupid girl thought they'd end up together. That lot are only out to take advantage of us, I'd tell her, and she'd answer back that I was living in the past. As if that nasty piece of work wasn't the very figure of his father. As if they hadn't led him to believe since he was a young boy that everything in this village was his for the taking.

I thought my daughter would get over all that nonsense when he came back to the village for a few days with his girlfriend, the one who ended up becoming his first wife.

A girl from Madrid, the daughter of one of the lawyers at the firm where he worked. Stuck-up and dry as a nun's tit, not a drop of charm and skinny as a rake. But nicely turned out and with private-school manners, even the way she had of walking like a countess, as if she'd paid for every paving stone on the street herself. He'd leave her at home with his mother and come sniffing around here for my daughter, but she refused to see him, she'd lock herself in the bedroom till he slunk off back down the road. He never came all the way to the door or rang the bell, but I'd know he was close because the whole house would shake. The walls would tremble and the air would turn so heavy you could barely breathe.

She was angry with him, but even more so with me. The women in this family have always spat our bile at each other till it wears through our insides. Back then I didn't know what my granddaughter has since told me, I was just angry that my daughter had been such an idiot, that she hadn't listened to me all those times I told her that the only thing those people want us for is to make and strip the beds, nothing else. She hated that I was right, that what I said would happen eventually happened. With each shouting match we had, the walls would shake and the wardrobe doors would start to open and shut. The ceilings creaked as if they were about to fall in, as if the roof were about to collapse onto our heads at any moment. But worst of all were the shadows. They'd grab at our ankles to trip us up, pull on our clothes and hang from our hair, throw the plates and cups from inside the cupboards at us. Our fights whipped them into a frenzy, they were driven mad by our ranting and raving, by our rot-in-hells and wish-you'd-never-been-borns.

Two weeks after Jarabo showed up in town with that hoity-toity girl, my daughter started going out with a local kid, a young bricklayer who hung out with a posse from Huete. I heard all about it from my saint, who climbed into bed with me one night. I remember she burnt the sheets with her halo and I had to throw them out. The brickie kid seemed very polite and hardworking, but my daughter didn't really like him, she was on the rebound and only dated him to make the Jarabo boy jealous. I hardly needed the saint to tell me that, I could see it for myself. The kid would turn up at the house looking for my daughter, sit on the stone bench out front waiting for her to come down, which sometimes wasn't for an hour. She never let me ask him in. I guess she was ashamed of me and the house, that she didn't want him seeing the scratched floors and yellow patches on the walls, the old dresses with shoddily stitched armholes and lopsided sleeves because, out of pure hatred for my mother, I'd never learnt to sew. When my daughter finally came down, the kid would gawp at her, mesmerised. Mouth hanging open and everything, the halfwit.

She dumped him almost straight away, after twenty days, as soon as the Jarabo boy went back to Madrid and she got bored of him shadowing her like a dog. He didn't take it well. He started following her around the village and showing up at the house. He'd linger by the door, trying to glimpse her through the curtains in the bedroom window. He wouldn't leave even when night fell. The house was on edge, fuelled by my daughter's worries, which grew with each passing day. Every time she looked out of the window she'd see him standing by the front gate, waiting. He began skipping work and barely slept, his mother was going around saying we'd sent him deranged, that he wasn't like that before he started going out with my daughter. I asked my girl to let me do something to get him off her back, but she wouldn't. Not so much as a little scare. She told me it was just him being stupid, that he'd soon get tired of it.

But he didn't get tired, they never do. Things went from bad to worse. One night the saint came and hovered by the kitchen ceiling as I was washing the pots and pans. She appeared to me there, her halo resplendent against the greasy yellow smoke stains. She told me my daughter was pregnant, that she was going to have a girl. I don't know how long I was off with her for, but it was dawn by the time I came to my senses.

The pregnancy was the talk of the village the second her bump started showing. Those damn gossips spoke of nothing else. They'd spent years wondering how I could have produced such a sweet, gorgeous girl, but now it all made sense. She was shameless like her mother, both of us knocked up after carrying on with boys like a pair of brazen hussies. So it turned out she did take after me.

That made her hate me even more. She'd always thought she was above me, that she'd snag a guy with a good job and get out of here, that she wouldn't have to set foot in this backwater again. But in the end she did exactly the same thing as me, and went and got pregnant too young. She blamed herself just like everyone in the village did, she thought she should have stopped him when he insisted. She hated herself for it and she hated me too because she saw herself reflected in me. She saw herself in ten years' time trapped in this same house with saggy clothes and a stupid child she'd never wanted.

I've always thought that was why she got back together with the bricklayer, so she wouldn't end up like me. Maybe she thought a crappy man was better than no man at all, and that he was her ticket out of here. I was eaten up with anger. I couldn't stand to see her back with that clown who'd spent days on end camped out in front of our house, spying on her like a lunatic. With men like that it's best to put some distance between you, before they put you in the ground.

For a while it seemed things were going well. They'd decided not to get married or live together till the baby was born, but he walked around town with her on his arm, as if she were his wife. He'd drive her to Cuenca to eat in nice restaurants, buy her bracelets and earrings that must have cost a pretty penny and which set chins wagging all through the village. And my daughter looked so gorgeous it hurt, even more beautiful now she was pregnant.

But when the girl was born that spring she kept playing for time. She stalled the wedding over and over again using any old excuse. The summer came around and she was back out with the boys when they returned to the village. She'd often not be home for days. The boyfriend would come looking for her, wild with jealousy, banging on the door. The baby would cry and the air in the house turned to oil.

The Jarabo boy had also returned for the holidays. This time he hadn't brought his girlfriend, but his mother had told everyone in the village they were planning their wedding for the following summer. That didn't seem to hold him back, and he kept meeting my daughter just like he'd always done, and she loved it. With a baby in the crib and a fiancé at the altar, the stupid girl still went chasing after the Jarabo boy the second he showed up in town. It made my guts rot. I didn't know which of them I hated more, or which was being more reckless.

When she did come home we'd hurl abuse at each other from the second she stepped through the door. They must have heard us all the way in the village. I'd tell her she was shameless for leaving her daughter for me to look after and going out gallivanting, and she'd snap back that at least it gave me something to do besides meddling in her life. I'd call her ungrateful and she'd call me crazy, I'd tell her it was going to turn out badly for her and she'd reply that she couldn't end up worse off than me. The baby girl would cry her eyes out, soaking up all that resentment, which had grown so much by then that the walls of the house actually bulged.

We argued the day she went missing as well, and the

Virgin knows I'll carry that knowledge to my deathbed. She stormed out, slamming the door so hard the house shook, and I didn't see her again till her shadow came knocking a few days later, but by then it was no longer her. Despite what my granddaughter says, I never found out which of the two men took her, and for all my begging the saints never told me. I carried the pain inside me for thirty years, like someone with a hole in their chest. But when my granddaughter helped me see things for how they really are, I understood that the saints hadn't told me a name because it didn't make any difference which of the two had done it. They'd each played their part and neither had paid for it. The shameless bastards were still alive and going around as if my daughter had never existed. One tied the knot with his fiancée the next summer, and the other married Emilia a couple of years later. They went on to have children as if they hadn't taken my child from me. As if I wasn't going to make them both pay.

9

They shed countless tears over the boy. The sound of the crying didn't reach this old pile of bricks, but then nothing ever does. Nothing makes it out of here and nothing gets in, either. Except the dead, of course, who haul their sorrows to the porch then grab hold of the doors, the walls and shelves, our hair and our ankles and whatever else they find. The living mostly steer clear unless they want to ask a favour or take us away, unless they're driven here by need or desperation.

The village women said you could hear the boy's mother crying at all hours, that day or night if you walked past the house you'd catch her muffled sobs. That's what Carmen told my grandma while I was listening from upstairs. The mother cried quietly, in that way rich people do, because bawling and keening is for plebs, for the people who make scenes and air their dirty laundry in public and don't know how to behave. She cried quietly but you could hear her all the same from the other side of the fence, from the street where locals walked by to eavesdrop, the women after some gossip to share in the fish queue and the men for fresh material for their mates in the bar.

When she went on TV she barely cried. She just sat there all posh and thin and young with her perfect clothes and her perfect make-up. And the things she said sounded so good, so private school, not a single muchismo instead of muchísimo or bonico instead of bonito. Every letter present and correct, one after another, and definitely no meltdowns. Her son had gone missing but she didn't make a fuss, didn't pull out fistfuls of her own hair or scream that she was going to rip the head off the animal who did it. She said her piece calmly and without raising her voice, without any threats or swearwords. You could see she was sad, her suffering was clear but she kept it all inside. A lone tear formed when she'd finished speaking, a tear that slid down her cheek and was elegantly dabbed dry before it reached her chin. That tear didn't make her mascara run or leave a smudgy line on her cheek because she wore the good stuff not the bargain-basement crap. When I used to go into her bathroom I'd stare at those little pots of powder that cost a month's wages. I'd see them there all neatly arranged and wonder how many months how many years I'd have to work to afford all that how much snot I'd have to wipe off her stupid brat and how many times I'd have to let him pull my hair to be worth as much as the contents of that make-up bag. How could I not stew as I looked at it all, how could my guts not eventually burst as I worked in that house and how could I not end up seeing things for how they really are?

I don't know what the mother said at the press conference, I heard the words coming out but I wasn't really listening. All I could take in was her perfect hair her perfect nails her perfect shirt. How many people were behind that image, how many underpaid lackeys with mortgages and monthly payments and houses full of roach traps and mould stains did it take to get her looking so perfect? The colourist for her hair, the manicurist for her nails, the maid to iron her clothes. And that's only counting that moment and not the years of beauty treatments the nannies she had as a girl and who never let her get her hands mucky the maids who for decades have spared her from unsightly grease and dust and shit the teachers who taught her to enunciate so well to express herself so well and never to break down in front of anyone not even when your son's gone missing because if you lose control and shout and swear and drop your consonants then no one will take you seriously. They'll feel sorry for you and say oh how dreadful the poor woman but take you seriously? Never.

I don't know what she said at the press conference but that wasn't the point, the point was to show people this was no ordinary family and the boy was no ordinary boy. That he had to be searched for high and low with no expense spared and everyone working overtime and extra resources brought in, that this wasn't one of those cases where you phone up the family when the trail goes cold and say we're doing all we can, we don't have any leads, we're ever so sorry, we'll keep an eye out, and then bury the file at the bottom of a drawer. This was the kind where there's trouble if you don't get results the kind where you might be phoned up by a judge or a government minister reminding you who calls the shots and what'll happen if the kid doesn't show up in case you'd forgotten how things work around here. The kind that's shown on TV day in day out and makes important people nervous, because those important people clock the manicured nails and cut-glass vowels and expensive clothes and they recognise one of their own.

This world wasn't made for those children to disappear, those children speak three languages before they start school but they don't disappear. The children who disappear are the ones whose mothers make scenes and rant and rave in the street and go on TV with unwashed hair, too shattered by grief to even shower and barely able to drag themselves out of bed. And the cameras film their greasy hair and shabby clothes and nails bitten to the quick from stress. They film these women in pieces, broken inside and out and they film their houses full of cheap furniture and old-fashioned curtains because they don't have two three four people taking care of everything for them or a lawyer to set up a press conference, an entire law firm to find a venue and invite the media and advise them on how to speak and how to move and what to say to the journalists circling like vultures for fodder for the endless TV debates. They don't have a lawyer or a maid or anything and everyone can see it and everyone feels sorry for them but everyone also understands that those children do disappear. They don't speak foreign languages and they've never been on a plane but they do disappear. No one wants them to and everyone thinks it's a shame but well maybe a tiny bit less of a shame since the press are quick to forget about them and pretty soon they're just a number within a statistic and everyone knows that's not a shame because no one feels bad about a number, you feel bad about the children with white skin and blonde hair when you know their favourite toy their favourite colour and the name of their little doggy.

The father was at the press conference too but he hardly said a word. He let his wife take centre stage because a crying mother is enough to break anyone but with a man it's different. When a man cries you feel something close to pity but not quite, more a creeping unease like hearing thunder when you're out in the woods. All men know that thing about crying mothers but if your own son goes missing you might forget and start sounding off at the police and the judges because you need to get the rage out somehow. But if you've got a lawyer or even a whole law firm on your side they'll make sure to position you behind the mother, tell you to hold her hand and not let go for the whole press conference and to slip in some sign of affection when she's finished speaking and a few words of thanks to law enforcement.

He obeyed on every count, he did everything right and on camera he even seemed younger, he even seemed handsome with that fancy tailored shirt and those curls he'd passed down to the boy. Anyone watching would have said his loving gesture was genuine, that he held his wife's hand every day and was worried about his son. I'd have thought so too, I'd have thought what a good father he was and how he must be going through hell because the tiniest gesture from a man will have everyone thinking he's father of the year. But I'd spent long enough in his house to know that he never even looked at the boy, and as for looking at the mother she was better off when he didn't. I'd also learnt that not even money can free you from men like that. Your family can own companies and annuities and land and apartments, but shitty men will come down on you all the same. I thought rich women had it easier with that stuff, that they just packed their bags and left, called a lawyer or two or three or four and got their ex-husband's cash but then I realised that no, that's not how it works, the men break them too, bit by bit, day after day, like someone digging a grave with a teaspoon. And when they screw up their courage and call a friend and say I can't take it anymore the friend tells them but if you walk out he won't pay you any maintenance you'll be alone with the boy and he'll have to change schools and then they call up their father and say I'm leaving and the father says don't cause a scene don't make trouble. Having money is always better. Money spreads everything with a nice layer of grease so that nothing squeaks and every-thing fits clickety-click into place, all the parts working like they're meant to, not splitting or snapping or stalling or crashing. We poor people spend our lives hammering parts that still never fit and meanwhile that lot haven't broken a sweat. But not even money can free you from men like that. That's what I saw in that house. Rich women also have to choose their men wisely 'cos even the ones you'd never expect can turn out to be the jealous type, the violent type who gets out his spoon on day one and cra-cracra keeps scraping till he's dug your grave.

I watched the press conference on my phone, in fits and starts because the connection kept cutting out. I wanted to see it but it wasn't like it made any difference to me what they said because the father had already given me his message, he'd already said he was going to ruin my life. Not him, of course, not personally. He wouldn't lower himself to coming out to his own maid's house. He had people for that, just like he had people for everything else. He sent the foreman, who's for exactly that, for yelling at the labourers when they talk or request their half-hour break or complain about their aches after hunching over the vines for ten hours straight.

The police hadn't yet arrested me at that point, they'd just questioned me for hours and made me repeat my story over and over since I'd been the one looking after the boy and the last person to see him. Not that it made any differ-ence to the father because to him I was still a maid who'd done a bad job and what he wanted was to give me a good thrashing. He wanted to drag me into the street and beat me to death or nearly to death because that's what you do with maids who slip up and spoil harvests businesses broodmares or children. I understand his rage, I get a father wanting to drag you around by the hair after you lose his son, but I also know he wouldn't have been so angry if the boy had been with family or friends when he went missing, that his rage was the rage of the master of the house whose servant's turned out to be a dud.

The foreman called out twice and was turning to leave when my grandma opened up and stood watching him from the doorway. The old girl would scare anyone with her hair flowing loose and her black dressing gown and piercing stare but he must have sensed something in the house as well because he glanced up at the little attic window and for a second his face crumpled. I was at the bedroom window and he didn't see me but I saw him and clearly noticed that flash of terror he tried and failed to hide. Maybe he saw something or maybe he felt the house wanting to pounce like an animal wild with hunger.

The father didn't send the foreman again but he must have made a few calls because he kept his promise all the same. The next day I was arrested and taken to prison. Maybe I got my story wrong but I doubt it because I'd repeated it so many times in my head and so many more in front of the police and I think I always said pretty much the same thing and the police never caught me in a lie. I don't think they had anything on me, but they arrested me to make it look like they were doing something. It had been six days and by then no one thought the boy would turn up alive or that he'd been kidnapped because such a small child wouldn't last long by himself and there'd been no call for a ransom. No one said it but everyone thought he was dead and everyone said he was dead behind closed doors but out in the street they said they mustn't give up hope, partly to convince themselves and partly in case word got back to the Jarabos.

They had to do something and they arrested me 'cos I

was an easy target and had no lawyer or contacts or friends in high places who could get me out of it. I had no money either so I stayed in prison till the lawyer they found me turned up, at which point the police had to let me go because they didn't have anything on me. But that was three months later and in all that time I only saw the lawyer once and only spoke to him on the phone once more. I did speak to the old woman though, to tell her not to come and see me because it would mean taking three buses and I was scared she'd get tired or pass out because though it's true she was doing well for her age, three buses are enough to make anyone feel faint and lose the will to live. I also told her not to leave the house because by now the whole village was convinced I'd killed the boy. She didn't listen to me but it's not like she went to the village much anyway. When she did leave the house it was only to wander out to the vegetable patch or look for the cats if she hadn't seen them for a few days in case they'd fallen down the ravine, or sometimes to remove the tapes hunters tied round the trees to mark the location of the hides. The one time she went down to the pharmacy everyone stared but no one said a word because people in this village are a mean, miserable lot, but most of all they're cowards.

No one said a word to her but everyone was talking about it. How could I not be guilty when no good had ever come from this house, when my mother was a brazen hussy who'd got knocked up and then walked out and never come back and when my grandma had bumped off her own husband over quarrels and bad blood? You only had to look at this family to see we were twisted, all widows and spinsters and no men around because none of them could hack it.

The press made everything worse by shoving mics in their faces and letting them tell all to the cameras and radio stations and anyone else who'd listen. More and more journalists turned up and the locals told them more and more details and the talk shows kept running the clip of that bitch from the butcher's calling my grandma demented because she showered naked in the garden and hid inside the wardrobes, and another video of that low-life grocer saying rumour had it she used the cats for casting spells and the bundles when someone went to ask a favour. And that really did get the old girl's back up because she didn't give a crap if people called her demented but she wouldn't stand for them saying she used those cats. She loved those kitties so much she called them master and ma'am, which she'd never have dreamed of doing for the Jarabos when she served in their house.

Not even my release shut those bigmouths up because the idea that I'd killed the boy had taken root inside them and now there was no weeding it out. The parents made another appearance, gave an interview at home, sitting up very straight on their living-room sofa, very well dressed and very much holding hands. The mother shed a few more tears this time and she even cried elegantly, without wrinkling her face or changing her expression. She looked thinner and more tired, not even that expensive make-up could cover the bags under her eyes. This time the father spoke as well to say that they trusted the police and the judges to do their job and knew they were working around the clock and that he and his wife still held out hope of finding their son alive. And if not, he said, looking straight at the camera, he'd make sure justice was done.

The interview carried on but I stopped watching because I knew that message was for me, that he was talking to me and me alone. Only this time instead of sending someone round he was saying it on TV for everyone to hear, so that his threat had witnesses and wouldn't get caught among the prayer cards hanging on the vine. When the TV channel posted the video online I watched it over and over, fast-forwarding and rewinding so he kept on saying he'd make sure justice was done. Again and again and again he said it. I burst out laughing every time. He could threaten me all he liked he could have me beaten up he could shoot me himself with his hunting rifle but it was never going to be justice. Justice was what we did when we made sure the boy wouldn't turn out like his parents or grandparents or great-grandparents and that the Jarabos' story ended there for good.

10

Those bastards came out with a pack of lies. Only a real ratbag would say I killed the cats to make my little bundles. Carmen put me on to it, after she saw it on the TV. Only a crawling heartless toad would say that, given how I keep those kitties, fur gleaming and looking like royalty. I never used to vaccinate them because that just wasn't done around here, but my granddaughter suggested it and now the vet comes by when we've got two cents to rub together and gives them the jab. He takes them off to be sterilised, too. That hasn't caught on here, either. Here people still stuff the newborn kittens in a sack and bash them to death like they always have.

If it wasn't for Carmen, I'd have stormed over to the grocer's and dragged that bigmouth across town by the last few greasy hairs on his head. What do you want, for the police to come and take you away like they did the girl? Carmen said. So I kept schtum to avoid making matters worse. I didn't drag the grocer across town but I did give him his just deserts. I prayed to the saint till my knees were red raw. Then the cold room stopped working over the weekend and all his fruit went bad. When he opened up on the Monday everything had gone mouldy, only the potatoes and onions could be salvaged.

My granddaughter thought that after her arrest no one would come to me for favours anymore, that they wouldn't want me doing their bundles or telling them if their dead relatives were lost or had been taken by the angels. But I know that band of fakes and two-faced creeps better than that. They're afraid of us now and yet they come knocking more than ever. Sometimes two or three will be hanging around by the door when night falls and I won't get to bed till well into the early hours. At the first whiff of their fear, the house starts creaking and shrieking. The shadows have come back so thick that sometimes one of our guests even sees them, just like you all do. They glimpse a dark form slinking over into a corner and look away without saying a word, even more scared than when they arrived. They also feel the cool air my daughter leaves behind when she passes them on the staircase or by the front door. It's always saddened me, my daughter leaving a chill like that.

After a few weeks the journalists disappeared and the pair of us wrapped up our unfinished business. For too long that other bastard had got away with what he did to my daughter. I could have dealt with him sooner, but the thought of not seeing her anymore also made me sad. I felt sure that the moment we handed him over to the shadows in the wardrobe, what remained of my daughter would leave and I'd never see her again, not even when I died, because I know that when I go I'll be staying right here within these four walls. Much as they come and hover in the kitchen now, the saints won't want to take me. A visit is one thing, but all eternity is quite another.

Eventually the police stopped coming back round here about the boy. And as for Emilia's husband, the bricklayer, they didn't find a single lead, and he was soon forgotten. The child's case remained open, but after a while not even the father's calls could prevent him falling into oblivion as well. At first the father had intimidated the police, then they'd felt sorry for him, and by the end he was a real thorn in their side. Carmen told me all this, she'd hear it around town and then come and relay it to me because she knew I'd lap it up. She also told me the mother rarely left the house. Gone were the visiting friends who admired their winery, gone were the trips to Madrid to spend on a handbag what my granddaughter earned in three months for putting up with that snot-nosed brat. Carmen used to say that when the mother went out she looked like a lost soul, skinny as a rake and head bowed.

Look, we may not have got their land off them, but we did bring them down a peg or two. Now, instead of respecting or fearing them, the locals pity them. They still have money because my saints can't do everything but where once people ran around after them like an idiot altar boy tailing the priest, now they snub them and give them a wide berth. Everyone knows that tragedy's catching and nobody wants it close. It digs in its claws and once it does I'd like to see anyone get them out.

In the end Carmen stopped coming and telling me things because she broke her hip and her nieces and nephews put her in a home, the same one as María, one of the cheapos because Carmen worked her entire life but had barely scraped together any pension. The Jarabos had never paid into a pot for her, at first because it wasn't the done thing, and later on because they couldn't be bothered. They told her they'd sack her if she kept insisting because, after all, she was getting on in years and they knew some Peruvian or Colombian girl would do the same job but for less, and without complaining. These days we speak on the phone but it's not the same because in the home she's turned all meek and musty and barely opens her mouth. When you think what she used to be like, you couldn't shut her up, and now getting three words out of her is like getting blood from a stone. I know she'll die of a broken heart. These days they call it depression but around here we've always called it dying of a broken heart. You notice a person stop going out, stop eating, basically lose the will to live, and before long they croak, and that's what's happening to Carmen. I hope she calls in to see me when she dies. I know the saints will take her because she never hurt a soul, and she was always helping others out. The only anger inside her was strictly reserved for the Jarabos and the police. I just hope she has time to pop over and say goodbye before they carry her off. I don't know if she guessed what happened to the boy because she never asked and I never told her. It would have been too heavy a burden to put on her when she'd had nothing to do with it. I'd like to tell her before she goes, but I'm afraid she'll end up trapped in this house if I do, if it stirs up her anger towards that family and then she no longer wants to leave.

It weighed heavily on my granddaughter, too, at first. She kept thinking the police would come for her at any moment and take her away again. At night in her dreams, she'd go over what she'd told them during the questioning. She'd also mutter something about the wardrobe, repeat what that rotten bastard had said while she'd led him by the arm up the stairs. I-don't-know-what-you're-talking-about, I-don't-know-what-you're-talking-about. I'd hear her repeat the same thing over and over as I lay in bed. She'd get up with a dry mouth and purple bags under her eyes, as if she hadn't slept a wink. When awake she wouldn't mention it, but I could see from her face that it was preying on her mind. She didn't leave the house and she barely ate. She'd spend all day lying on the wooden bench and her eyes would glaze over and I'd know she was back to brooding again. The unease had burrowed deep down into her guts and now it wouldn't budge. I was afraid it'd stay inside her and she'd let herself fade away like Carmen.

One night I woke her up when she was talking in her sleep and made her get out of bed. I couldn't stand it any longer. Every night she'd keep me up, drive me half mad with those lines she muttered non-stop through gritted teeth. She'd be asleep but I'd be wide awake since there was no way I was getting any shut-eye with her wittering on like that. That night I woke her up and it was more like I was pulling her from the bottom of a well than from a dream. She was sweating and trembling feverishly and when she opened her eyes she looked at me as if she'd never seen me before and had no idea where she was. Her mouth was full of thick white spittle that had formed crusts at the corners of her mouth and the bags under her eyes were deeper and darker than ever.

I grabbed her hand and pulled her over to the wardrobe on the other side of the room. I couldn't stand it any longer, we were both going to lose our minds. The wood creaked and the door opened slightly. I could feel how hungry it was. I asked my granddaughter to help me push the wardrobe away from the wall. It was heavy as hell, as if full of rocks. It didn't want to be moved. Then I crouched down by the wall and counted the bricks, running my finger over them. I couldn't remember the last time I'd done this, but it must have been many years ago, before my granddaughter was born. For a long time I checked every week to see if my father had moved, until I realised he was never getting out of there. We women couldn't get out of the trap he'd laid for us, but neither could he.

I pushed the brick gently at one end, then carefully teased it out. The old plaster crumbled and some of it fell to the floor. My granddaughter watched me, her eyes glassy with sleep, not really understanding what I was doing. After taking a quick look inside I stood up and leant against the wall because my knees were aching like sin. I handed her the torch I keep in the drawer of my nightstand in case of power cuts, because in this house it's not a good idea to be left completely in the dark.

She took the torch and knelt down without saying a

word. I don't know if by that point she'd come back from the hole she'd sunk into while she slept but the expression on her face had changed. She was still sweating but now her jaw was clenched. She brushed aside the hair stuck to her brow and switched on the torch. A tremor ran through the house. Downstairs the doors clattered open and shut and the pots and pans crashed against the kitchen floor. It had been a while since there'd been a racket quite like that. Sometimes they might dare throw a knife or fork left lying on the table or open a cupboard a little way, but they hadn't made that kind of scene in a long time.

She poked the torch through the hole in the brickwork and moved her face closer, shining the light from side to side till she spotted him. I knew she'd seen him because she jumped slightly, but then she moved her face even closer. Her damp hair had bits of loose plaster sticking to it. She ran the beam of the torch across the three figures. The biggest was still propped in the same place as always, his mouth hanging open and his eye sockets empty. Beside him was another, also a man. It was clear he'd been there for much less time, the house hadn't yet totally consumed him. The third figure was barely a metre tall. He was leaning against the wall with his legs stretched out in front and his hands flopped by his sides. His eyes were closed.

My granddaughter moved away from the wall and put the brick back where it had been. She turned off the torch, got up from the floor, brushed the dust from her pyjama bottoms and the plaster from her hair. The house had fallen silent. The only sound came from the cats out in the garden. They never slept inside when it was hot. We pushed the wardrobe back into place. Then we each climbed into our separate beds and I switched off the bedside lamp.

Acknowledgements

To my maternal grandmother, for letting me tell the story of her house and her family. For explaining the saints' lives to me and teaching me to listen to them. For talking to me about the dead who appear in a corner of the bedroom. To my mother, for believing in revenge. To my father and brother, because I know they're proud of this story even if they won't say so. To Sara and Munir, for being my first readers. To Victoria, my editor, for the corrections and the help, but most of all for believing in this novel. To José, because ever since I told him over the phone that my great-grandfather 'lived off women', he's been part of the story that's told in this book, and part of my story as well.

THE LEOPARD

The leopard is one of Harvill's historic colophons and an imprimatur of the highest quality literature from around the world.

When The Harvill Press was founded in 1946 by former Foreign Office colleagues Manya Harari and Marjorie Villiers (hence Har-vill), it was with the express intention of rebuilding cultural bridges after the Second World War. As their first catalogue set out: 'The editors believe that by producing translations of important books they are helping to overcome the barriers, which at present are still big, to close interchange of ideas between people who are divided by frontiers.' The press went on to publish from many different languages, with highlights including Giuseppe Tomasi di Lampedusa's *The Leopard*, Boris Pasternak's *Doctor Zhivago*, José Saramago's *Blindness*, W. G. Sebald's *The Rings of Saturn*, Henning Mankell's *Faceless Killers* and Haruki Murakami's *Norwegian Wood*.

In 2005 The Harvill Press joined with Secker & Warburg, a publisher with its own illustrious history of publishing international writers. In 2020, Harvill Secker reintroduced the leopard to launch a new translated series celebrating some of the finest and most exciting voices of the twenty-first century.

Pedro Almodóvar: *The Last Dream*
    trans. Frank Wynne
Laurent Binet: *Civilisations*
    trans. Sam Taylor
Paolo Cognetti: *The Lovers*
    trans. Stash Luczkiw
Paolo Cognetti: *Without Ever Reaching the Summit*
    trans. Stash Luczkiw
Pauline Delabroy-Allard: *All About Sarah*
    trans. Adriana Hunter
Álvaro Enrigue: *You Dreamed of Empires*
    trans. Natasha Wimmer
Urs Faes: *Twelve Nights*
    trans. Jamie Lee Searle
María Gainza: *Portrait of an Unknown Lady*
    trans. Thomas Bunstead
Stefan Hertmans: *The Ascent*
    trans. David McKay
Mayumi Inaba: *Mornings With My Cat Mii*
    trans. Ginny Tapley Takemori
Ismail Kadare: *A Dictator Calls*
    trans. John Hodgson
Ismail Kadare: *The Doll*
    trans. John Hodgson
Jonas Hassen Khemiri: *The Family Clause*
    trans. Alice Menzies

Karl Ove Knausgaard: *In the Land of the Cyclops: Essays*
    trans. Martin Aitken
Karl Ove Knausgaard: *The Morning Star*
    trans. Martin Aitken
Karl Ove Knausgaard: *The Wolves of Eternity*
    trans. Martin Aitken
Karl Ove Knausgaard: *The Third Realm*
    trans. Martin Aitken
Antoine Leiris: *Life, After*
    trans. Sam Taylor
Édouard Louis: *A Woman's Battles and Transformations*
    trans. Tash Aw
Édouard Louis: *Change: A Method*
    trans. John Lambert
Geert Mak: *The Dream of Europe: Travels in the Twenty-First Century*
    trans. Liz Waters
Layla Martínez: *Woodworm*
    trans. Sophie Hughes & Annie McDermott
Haruki Murakami: *First Person Singular: Stories*
    trans. Philip Gabriel
Haruki Murakami: *Murakami T: The T-Shirts I Love*
    trans. Philip Gabriel
Haruki Murakami: *Novelist as a Vocation*
    trans. Philip Gabriel & Ted Goossen
Ngũgĩ wa Thiong'o: *The Perfect Nine: The Epic of Gĩkũyũ and Mũmbi*
    trans. the author

Kristín Ómarsdóttir: *Swanfolk*
   trans. Vala Thorodds
Intan Paramaditha: *The Wandering*
   trans. Stephen J. Epstein
Per Petterson: *Men in My Situation*
   trans. Ingvild Burkey
Andrey Platonov: *Chevengur*
   trans. Robert Chandler & Elizabeth Chandler
Mohamed Mbougar Sarr: *The Most Secret Memory of Men*
   trans. Lara Vergnaud
Dima Wannous: *The Frightened Ones*
   trans. Elisabeth Jaquette
Emi Yagi: *Diary of a Void*
   trans. David Boyd & Lucy North